Nikki Chronicles

an erotic novel

Cherayla

Nikki Chronicles

Editor: *Sasha Ravae, Black Eden Publications*
Cover Designer: *Niyah Solomon, Black Eden Designs*

United States:
10 9 8 7 6 5 4 3 2 1

Acknowledgements

To my partner, Stephan—you inspire me in innumerable ways. Thank you for choosing to love me every day. My children Papi, Ar, and Pooh, I love you so much…and you better not sneak and read this until you are grown!

Mama, your desire to support me beyond understanding is not unseen. Dr. Nicole Price—the Blueprint—your encouragement has been as important as your example.

Shaun Brown, wifey, you know why. Lanesha Frazier, Courtney Richardson, Michelle Greene, Leandrea Mack, who knew your Juneteenth session would lead me to this?

Black Eden Publications, your feedback and editing was exactly what I needed. I am so grateful for our work relationship.

One Mic KC, Soul Sessions KC, Natasha Ria El-Scari for the first round of editing, thank you.

Finally, my gratitude to the Creator for all things, for the gift. Love to the ancestors for my fortitude, and courage to my legacy to do the things that scare you.

—Cherayla

One

"So, you went to college?" Darrell looked at me with one eyebrow raised.

"Yes," I said with a flip of my hair.

"Which one?"

"You've never heard of it—it's a small school in Missouri."

"Try me..."

He still didn't believe me.

"...Roosevelt University."

I knew this New Yorker had never heard of Roosevelt. Hell, he'd never even met someone from Kansas City before, but I could sense this was a test. And as the fine-ass manager of Dream—the club I was currently working at—I felt obligated to inform Darrell that I was *not* a dumb broad. I had a college degree and *chose* to be here because I like it.

I liked the attention, the fast (non-taxable) money, the dancing...really all of it—except the groping. Like when some dude who digs ditches for a living tries to grab you by the pussy just because he thinks he's entitled to your body. Oh, and dumb dudes...most men are completely oblivious to the world around them (despite who runs the world). Half these guys wouldn't know the three branches of government if the tree grew right in their front yard. So, having conversations with them was like watching paint dry.

Like I said, I chose to be here, and I do like it…but I don't *love* it, and I have rules.

I don't dance nude. The only people who should see my vaginal cavity are my gynecologist and whoever is lucky enough to enter into my love cave.

I'm not a whore, and I don't sleep with customers no matter how much they spend or "offer" to spend. I hate the propositions; I just like to dance—for money. Don't get me wrong, I love sex—*a lot*—with whoever I want at the time. And honestly…right now, I wanted Darrell bad, and whatever Nikki wants, Nikki gets.

I'd been going over this conversation mentally for a few days now, and I was so sure that he was interested in me, but he hadn't said a word about it.

Tonight was another slow night.

"…I looked up Roosevelt College, Nikki…or should I say, *[redacted]*?" Darrell said, walking up behind me.

Ah. My name...I should discuss that briefly before we continue. Do you really *need* to know my government name? I mean, the story is the most important thing, isn't it?

Let's just stick with my stage name—Nikki—and know that all other names have been changed to protect the innocent. This is *my* story, but I'm not sure how much of it will affect my real life, so I need to keep some things to myself.

I smiled at the mispronunciation of my government name; he had clearly done his research. I was a recent graduate from Roosevelt and was heavily involved in extracurricular activities, so my face was plastered all over their website.

After correcting his pronunciation, I said, "It's actually Roosevelt *University,* not College. Don't disrespect my alma mater." Turning toward him with bedroom eyes, I asked, "Are you impressed?"

He nodded slowly, swirling his water with lemon. Leaning in close, I stood in-between his legs and felt his breath on my neck as my lips touched his ear.

"My brain is the most attractive thing about me, but I could impress you with *so* much more."

He stopped stirring his drink, and I could sense him attempting to catch his breath. It was barely noticeable, just enough of a reaction to show he heard me.

I wore a white thong with neon green chaps and a neon blue bikini top that barely hid my perfect teardrop-shaped titties. I had a great smile, and my body wasn't too shabby—I had a flat stomach and an ass that made shopping for jeans a constant problem.

I could tell that Darrell didn't really care about the condition of my ass though.

Looking like Latto and sounding like Angela Rye was a combination he couldn't resist—and I didn't want him to. He needed to be inside of me. This pussy could change his life!

After rubbing his back for a moment, I sauntered away to go talk to a potential customer.

Darrell and I flirted on slow nights, but, honestly, I had been lusting after him ever since the day I turned in my application. I mean, *immediately*. He was definitely a zaddy, and I was trying to find out all about him.

Through conversation, I had discovered that he was a lawyer by trade, but no longer practiced, lived right outside the city, had two daughters, loved his mama, and had just gone through a divorce. I could tell that he was older than me, but the light in the club made it difficult to gauge his real age. But tonight, I just asked him flat-out.

"I'm…35," he smirked.

“35? Wow,” I laughed, not believing a word of it.

He must’ve said it so many times that it had to be true. But based on the music he mentioned he grew up listening to, I knew he was in his 40s, but I let him rock with that answer.

I knew in my heart he was lying, but I didn’t really care. Darrell was smart, dressed like a man with money (regular jeans, expensive understated shoes, button-up shirts, and Bond No. 9 cologne). He was 6’5, the color of wet sand, and thick as hell. He looked like he played sports back in college with his broad shoulders and defined arms. Occasionally, he would come in with only a t-shirt and jeans on, and his pecs were popping like he did a hundred pushups every night but didn’t give a damn about sit-ups. He had the body of a man who used to workout often but now he found himself eating good. He had the kind of belly that could slap against your clit when it got good in bed. Plus, it didn’t hurt that he drove a cocaine white 745 BMW—Rick Ross lyrics played in my mind every time I saw him in it, and my pussy would tingle a little too. I constantly daydreamed about playing with his dick while we rode along the West Side Highway. Damn, he was fine.

I danced on weekdays to avoid paying tip out on weekends. Dream was a new club, and a lot of the girls only wanted to work when they thought all the ballers would be out. Management allowed as many girls to dance as the club could hold; then they made them pay *egregious* tip outs just for the opportunity to dance at their club.

Tip outs, or “house fees,” were a travesty—a way for club owners to pimp out the dancers and cover their asses if the bar didn’t make any money. Most nights, tip out was $40-$50. But whenever there was a big party, tip out increased because they knew dancers were making a ton of money.

To avoid tip out completely, I agreed to work a few weekdays, so there were actual dancers in the building every night they were open. Even though it was slow, some of your favorite rappers or athletes would pop-in wanting to be incog-negro on a random Wednesday night. They often wanted a private dance, a drink, (or a bottle), and then they'd dip. Sometimes, those were the best nights because they weren't trying to be all big and bad and show out for anybody. They paid in big bills, not wanting to wait for change, and would just be cool. Dream was not a big place; it was very intimate and easy for someone high profile to sneak in and out—and they often did!

One of the owners was an old school rapper named Hieroglyphics, or "Hyro" as we called him, with one *huge* hit that Erykah Badu had sampled, making the song even bigger. He had relationships with porn stars and other dancers around the country because of that song, so he parlayed his money into a New York strip club.

Hyro was cool as a fan and super chill. He was also happily married to this gorgeous woman who sometimes came in to visit him. None of the dancers had any idea what his dick was like because he kept it to himself—you gotta respect a man with integrity like that, and we did.

Whenever Hyro talked about "rules," he always mentioned his "silent investor," who was always watching to be sure operations went smoothly. All us girls had bets on who this "silent investor" was. Sometimes, guesses would get outrageous.

One night, somebody guessed Bill Gates; another guess was Jesse Jackson. (Yes, *the* Jesse Jackson.) As time went on, our guesses got more fantastic, but Hyro would just laugh, never revealing the truth.

As far as the "rules" went, they were basically the same everywhere in non-nude clubs, but these were posted in our dressing room *everywhere*. We were expected to know them and use them…or suffer higher tip-outs or possibly be barred from ever working there again.

THE RULES:

1. **WALK INTO WORK LOOKING LIKE MONEY—A CUSTOMER COULD BE LURED IN BY YOUR LOOKS.** You may have a potential customer for life just by who you met on the train. Inviting him to the club you work at sounds kinda cheesy, but I've met plenty of people that way…and believe me they *pay!*

2. **KEEP IT CLEAN IN VIP—NO EXCEPTIONS!** Undercover cops try gaining your trust. Sometimes, they work for weeks at a time to break you down. And once they have you in VIP, they will ask you to "pull it to the side" or to "touch it just this once." And after they finish and the money is in your hands, they will *then* arrest you for prostitution. Cold world. [1]

3. **WASH YOUR ASS AND BRING PUM-PUM WIPES WITH YOU TO WORK.** Baby wipes

[1] Nude dancing or any form of a sexual act is illegal in public settings in New York City. In fact, dancing in public bars was considered illegal until 2018 due to the Cabaret Law. (Look it up!)

are cool, but those vagina wipes are a godsend on the nights you're really working and sweating down there. Don't have the club smelling like a fish market.

4. **DON'T GIVE OUT YOUR NUMBER—KEEP THE FANTASY ALIVE.** If you give out your number to everybody who spends money on you, what is the point of coming to the club? You have to keep some kind of mystery and keep them coming back to see you. In other words, if they can see you *out*side, they won't spend money *in*side.

5. **LISTEN FOR YOUR NAME ON THE STAGE ROTATION AND ADHERE TO IT.** If you ignore the DJ calling your name 3x in one night, you won't hit the stage for a month. For some, this is no big deal. Half these girls can't dance anyway—they make more money working the floor and in VIP than on stage. But on the nights when the ballers walk in, you want to be seen because they throw money at anything on stage, and you could miss out on easy money just because you ignored the DJ.

6. **LET THE DOORMAN WALK YOU TO YOUR VEHICLE OR TAXI. DON'T LEAVE ALONE.** Self-explanatory. The same dudes (and ladies) believed the fantasy you created, and still could be living in that fantasy after the club closes, wanting to make you into their personal dancer—at their house, with their *other* toys.

Don't be a toy. Stay alive and let security walk you out.

7. **DON'T EVER LEAVE WITH A CUSTOMER.** This one is a little tricky because girls leave with customers *all* the time—even if it's just to get a ride to the train station. Nowadays, it's a lot easier to leave with customers without anyone noticing because of all the rideshare services—they can pretend to be one, and you just hop in the backseat. But it's still discouraged. **See Rule #4.**

8. **DON'T DATE ANY OF THE DREAM STAFF. IF YOU ARE DISCOVERED DATING, ONE OF YOU WILL BE FORCED TO RESIGN.** By "date," they really mean, "don't fuck any of the Dream staff." But in reality, half the dancers have fucked the bouncers *and* the DJ. I think this rule is just there to look good. But me? I don't shit where I eat, so I have never…plus, most of these niggas were raggedy anyway. Darrell was the exception—he was my unicorn.

9. **GIVE RESPECT TO ALL YOUR CO-WORKERS.** AKA, don't start fights in the locker room. Don't steal customers. Don't steal money. Don't steal perfume. Don't steal clothes. (Yuck!) Everybody here is not your friend, but you can be friendly*!*

A dancer named Cocoa got real buddy-buddy with me once. She was an O.G., but one night, I let her use my locker because she had forgotten her lock. I heard them call her name to the stage, and she came prancing out of the locker room with one of my biggest money-making outfits on. I could not believe she was so grimy!

I could sense the other girls looking at me to see what I was going to do, especially since I was always telling them that fighting wouldn't solve anything. So, I calmly walked into the locker room, removed her items, folded them, and put them inside locker #17. Then, I went to the DJ's booth and had him announce that there were free clothes inside locker #17.

The girls rushed to the back and grabbed every stitch of Cocoa's outfits, even the clothes she had come to work in. She had to go home in a *Club Dream* t-shirt and stripper heels. I still chuckle to this day because I know how petty I am. The point is that I can get my point across without fighting, and I generally do.

10. **KEEP YOUR MONEY TO YOURSELF.** People steal. Even good people find easy money hard to resist. It's easier to remove temptation completely and be responsible with your own money. Change out your singles frequently so your knot looks smaller. New York dancers carry purses, but Southern dancers always carry their money on their garter belts. Since I came up in the dance world from Florida, my money is always on me. A purse is cool for aesthetics, but it's easily stolen. If a bitch is bad enough to steal off my leg, she deserves that money—she earned it!

*****

After finding out my real name a few weeks ago, Darrell and I were chatting more frequently at the bar—flirting heavily, but never crossing any lines. Tonight had been super slow as usual, with no real customers in sight, so we were closing a little early. And Darrell asked me to come to his office after I got dressed.

Dancers *never* get asked to come to the office, so immediately, my sex antennas started beeping, and I started throbbing as I made my way to the dressing room.

Oh, my god, we are about to break Rule #8...and at work! That is. So. Fucking. Hot. I'm so glad G. Money wasn't available last night.

So much for that sneaky link. Darrell was gonna get this tight, wet, throbbing pussy instead.

When I got undressed, there was a thin layer of that clear, slimy moisture in my thong…the kind I got when I was *highly* stimulated, and I knew it was because of Darrell. It most definitely wasn't the money I made tonight.

I should have worn a miniskirt today; instead, I wore a jogging suit with a crop top and a push-up bra. I planned to leave my bra off for easy access, but if I left my panties off, I was afraid that I'd leak through my pants accidentally. This wet-wet was real, okay?

I intentionally took a long time to get ready, allowing the other dancers to exit and hopefully have the entire club to myself—well, ourselves.

Doing my best sexy walk out of the dressing room, I saw Darrell, Rob the security guard, and Peaches (another dancer) all waiting in the hallway.

"Damn, girl, what took you so long?" Peaches laughed, throwing her bag over her shoulder.

"I figured you could use a ride home to save money on cab fare since it was so slow tonight. We all are going Uptown, so wassup…?" Darrell asked. I could tell he wasn't flirting. It was as if none of the flirting we had done had even happened.

Now, I was shaking my head, calling myself a "fool" for thinking we would actually break Rule #8 here at the club. I was kicking myself for being too caught up.

"Oh, okay, let me call you a cab then," Darrell said, obviously confused by my vigorous head shaking.

"No, no, I mean, 'yes.' *Yes,* I would love a ride…home, that is. All of you live Uptown too…? Dag, I didn't know."

Rob grabbed the passenger's seat of Darrell's luxury vehicle, and Peaches and I took the back. I pouted all the way to the car. I hadn't been this disappointed since the Migos broke up.

Peaches was a gorgeous, 5'7, dark-skinned goddess. Her measurements were 38-27-43, and her thighs were strong like a wrestler's. She had dark almond-shaped eyes and sexy lips that made her a customer favorite—the only thing was…she could not dance. She had no rhythm at all and loved the fact that she would go month after month not hitting the stage. In fact, that rule may have been made specially to benefit her instead of punishing the rest of us. Some people are sexy no matter what they do. Like, take me for instance…I'm attractive, but I have to *try* to be "sexy." Peaches' sexiness oozed out of her so effortlessly that men were drawn to her like bees to honey.

Rob was an overly aggressive Iraq War veteran suffering from undiagnosed PTSD. He wasn't who I would have chosen for security, but I guess somebody owed him a favor.

His conversation was always limited, and he somehow had radar for inappropriate customers. This guy tried to touch my pussy once, and Rob put him in a chokehold before I could give him a gentle reprimand. Unfortunately, he never came back. That guy was a good tipper too. I could have told him in a way that would've stopped his behavior if given the chance for correction. Anyway, Rob had a rotten tooth on the side that made him hold his jaw in a weird way—the stench emanating from his mouth while the windows were rolled-up in the car was like a dumpster fire. If you've ever smelled a rotten tooth, you know it's atrocious. And you can't escape it, not even for a moment. But yet and still, Rob was animatedly discussing last night's basketball game with Darrell.

"Darrell, may I crack the window a little?" I asked, sweetly.

"Nikki, it's 34 degrees outside," he chuckled.

"Is that a 'no'?"

"If you must," he licked his lips. This time, he looked straight at me in the rearview mirror before he quickly took over the conversation. "How'd you two make out tonight?"

"It was dead tonight, but I made a little somethin' somethin'," Peaches said.

"I personally would have preferred to be dancing at $20 a song, but I made a little money," I chimed in. "So, it's all good."

Darrell glanced in the rearview again.

"Nik, I noticed you changed clothes from what you had on earlier."

My cheeks flushed as my mind began to race. *Did he notice what I was wearing when I walked in tonight? Why would he make a comment like that if he isn't feeling me?* The only thing that changed was the removal of my bra, so my nipples instantly perked up.

Darrell licked his lips again.

"Yeah, I just wanted to be ready for anything that happens tonight, you know?" I glanced into the mirror trying to give my sexiest eye, but my lash glue was coming undone, so I had to blink a few times and swat it away.

I caught Darrell laughing a little as he continued to look at me in the mirror and I had to laugh too. At that moment, I realized that I needed to be around Darrell outside of work in another environment, and it had to be tonight.

"Y'all tryna go out to eat? I'm starving." I was trying to buy some more time.

Rob and Peaches exchanged looks before they both just shrugged.

"Sure."

"That's a great idea, Nik," Darrell smiled. "My treat, y'all."

Two

At 2 a.m. on a Wednesday headed Uptown, the best place for a group of people to go for food was Starlight Diner. It was so old that it had likely been there since the Harlem Renaissance. Hell, it had probably been there since the Statue of Liberty was brought over from France.

Starlight Diner was a New York institution. The floor was slick with years of old grease that had been mopped over with old, cold, murky water so every step off the mat could be a "man down" situation.

"Oh, shit!" I shouted as my feet went out from under me. Case in point, I had slipped just two steps inside the door.

Darrell grabbed my waist and steadied me quickly. His breath on my neck smelled like a green apple Jolly Rancher.

"Are you okay? You have to be careful."

"Yes, thank you. I forgot how slippery this floor is...but, hey! You had Jolly Ranchers and didn't offer me one?"

Darrell laughed his signature, quiet laugh, despite having such a loud presence.

"You smelled my breath over the fried onions, bacon, and fried meats in the air? Are all your senses that strong?"

Looking back at him, I wondered if this was a moment, but I just wasn't sure. He was sending me so many mixed signals, I just couldn't tell what was up with him.

Running through the possible list of reasons he wasn't trying harder to get with me, I thought, *One, he has a girlfriend. Two, he's not feeling me like I thought he was. Three, he's just a friendly guy, or four, he was a real stickler for rules.*

Whatever the reason, I couldn't get a read on him, and it had me hyped! The fact that he was playing games made my toxic-ass want him even more.

Working in a strip club, part of my job was to come-on to men. That was part of the beauty of these places—the status quo was flipped. In the "real" world, heterosexual women are expected to be approached and pursued by men. But in the strip club world, the roles are naturally reversed—as women are working to try and part men from their money. Don't get me wrong…there are plenty of men who pursue the dancers, but they're generally just trying to have sex with them, not grow a relationship or even spend money on them, honestly.

Anyway, Darrell never talked to anyone else more than he did me. That, I could tell. I never saw him involved in conversation with anyone. There was no doubt that he was feeling me, but he was playing games. Little did he know, I was a master at 2K!

Darrell sat beside me in the booth, and Peaches and Rob sat across from us. We all started cracking jokes immediately—on the other people there, on each other, on the customers who came to the club. I was crying laughing.

Darrell went to pull his phone out. His hand brushed against my hip, and I was grateful that I had decided to wear panties, or there would've been a puddle underneath me. What was it about him that made me soaking wet like this?

I leaned into him when he put his phone back into his pocket, and he gratefully left his hand on my knee as he kept cracking jokes.

Allowing it to linger, the weight of his hand was like Black Lightning had touched me—a soft current of electricity flowed directly from his hand into my knee, up my thigh, around my ass, and straight to my pussy. Was this dude a secret superhero?!

I barely noticed that he was pulling my right thigh toward his, until I felt my inner thighs were no longer touching. Little by little, he was cranking my legs open.

By the time the food arrived, I could barely breathe.

Darrell had used his hand to open my legs slowly, softly, but with tenacity until, eventually, my right knee was touching his left one. At that moment, I realized how powerful his touch was.

It only increased the spark between us. And I could've sworn I was buzzing. I had so much electricity running through my body, I could've started a car. Was this validation for what I was feeling between us? Or was he still playing games…?

Once Darrell picked up his fork and knife and tore into his chicken salad, I assumed that the "game" was over. No longer feeling the spark between us, I began to close my legs, but he gently parted them again. In the midst of telling jokes, I tried over and over again to close my legs—but when he felt that my knee was not on his, he would reach under the table again and gently pull it toward him.

This seemingly simple non-verbal request/demand to submit to his will made my breath quicken and my cheeks flush. The sheer control he had over me was so sickeningly attractive that I could barely eat my food.

Finishing his salad before the rest of us and popping a mint in his mouth, Darrell had his hand back on my knee. He moved it further and further up my thigh until he was tracing my panty line with his forefinger, and I was afraid I was going to die of attraction—was that even possible?

Darrell smiled as he cupped my entire pussy with his left-hand, feeling my wetness through my pants. He started moving his hand like he was waving goodbye, with the brunt of his palm rubbing my sweet spot slowly.

Catching my breath, I opened my legs wider for him to have more access—but he just stopped before he stood up.

"It looks like everyone is done, and I already paid. Let's get outta here."

…and I was left gasping for air.

Peaches looked worried.

"Nik, are you okay? You look like you just saw a ghost."

"Yes, I-I-I'm fine—just had a wave come over me," I stuttered, trying to pull my thoughts and my pum-pum together all at the same time.

"A wave? What kind of wave?" she pressed, laughing.

"I'm just tired is all. Let's go."

We took our same seats in Darrell's car, and as conversation carried on from the restaurant, I didn't hear a thing. I was too lost in my own fantasies. I was also hoping that the dark of night could cover up the fact that my pants may have had a wet stain on them from the intense sexual encounter I just had. Nobody, and I mean *nobody* had ever done anything like that to me before. And I wasn't no square! I'd had my fair share of crazy sex encounters, but this was on some other shit.

I took a break from my daydream to look up into the rearview mirror. I could feel Darrell staring at me.

"Nik, are you okay?" he asked, snapping me out of my thoughts. Peaches started laughing.

"Damn, girl, you really must be tired."

"You said, '7th between 144th and 145th,' right? Are you on the east or west side of the street?" Darrell questioned.

I realized we were almost at my house

Is he dropping me off first? Damn.

We pulled up, and Darrell dropped me off without a second look.

"Have a good night, Nik," he said over his shoulder. "See you later this week."

Needing to release my frustration, after setting my things down in my room, I went to take a shower.

As the water cascaded over my skin, I thought long and hard about what Darrell had done to my body. With my wet, soapy, hands, I began rubbing my neck, nipples, and stomach. Once I rinsed off, I ventured down to my pussy; I touched her in disbelief that she was still throbbing...and then I began to rub her in a circular motion, increasing intensity until I had finished the job Darrell had started.

After lotioning up, I went to sleep dreaming of cumming on his fingers.

*****

By Friday, I was so busy grinding on crotches and swinging on the pole that I barely noticed Darrell looking at me over his ginger ale. Darrell rarely drank on the job, and like me, he wanted to keep a level-head at all times when it came to the money. I didn't *ever* wanna be in a situation where my money was in question because of some liquor. So, when men offered to buy me a drink—which they often did—the bartender knew my drink of choice. I paid them every night to mix up a drink in advance for me—cranberry juice and ginger ale with a splash of grenadine added at the end for effect. The customers never knew, and I even took shots of this non-alcoholic concoction.

Whenever a customer insisted that I drink whatever they're drinking, I always end up "accidentally" spilling it…or I just give it to the bartender to take. (They drink like fish anyway, so it was no big deal).

If I weren't already mostly naked at this point in a leopard-print bra and thong, I would've thought that Darrell was undressing me with his eyes.

Walking into VIP for a private dance, I looked back at him and winked. My pussy was throbbing so much that I couldn't wait to shake my ass for this little funky $50. All this pent-up sexual energy made for the best dance of that boring-ass accountant's life. All the while, I was pretending that I was fucking Darrell. Every time I stood up, I licked my lips slowly at the camera. I knew he was watching on the monitors in the back office. I couldn't prove it, but I felt it in my soul.

As I walked out of VIP with my customer, Darrell was charging out of the back office so fast that I knew my suspicions were correct—he was watching, and I loved knowing that his eyes were on me.

Although we didn't speak all night, he continued to follow me with his eyes…watching all my customer interactions. I felt like a fool waiting around at closing time for him to offer me a ride home again, especially since it didn't look like any such offer was coming.

But the feeling of disappointment was short-lived since I had a pocketful of money, and thanks to our biggest money makers Ariel and Dimples getting kicked out for fighting, I made *wayyyy* more money than I normally would've. They were literally *always* fighting over some dude named Jerome. Apparently, Jerome had a dick made of gold because neither of them could really claim him. Word was he was married to a woman out in Jersey but kept a harem of strippers at his beck and call. There was so much good dick out in the world, Lord only knows why they fought over him every other week.

Due to their absence, I worked extra hard and skipped out of the club with my pocket full of money, before hailing a cab nearby. I peeped a cocaine white BMW 745 pull out from a side street—the driver rolled the window down and asked if I needed a ride.

Oh, hell no!

Darrell had basically ignored me all night; plus, he could've asked me if I needed a ride while we were both *in*side the club. Pulling up beside me *out*side the club made me feel like a prostitute.

My pride wouldn't allow me to accept anything from him now.

"You think I'm some kind of hoe or something, getting picked up off the street? No, thank you!"

He smiled.

"No problem, *[redacted]*. I'll see you later. You can count on that," he said before he pulled off.

My dumbass was really catching a taxi home instead of getting a ride with a man I wanted inside of me more than anything else. Standing there stuck, trying to hail a cab, I was kicking myself for being so bullheaded, but what else was I supposed to do? I couldn't allow him to see how weak I was for him, that he could lowkey play me all night, and I would just fold. Fuck that!

I put my cab money in one hand and my tips from the night in the other. I was so tired by the end of the night, I fell asleep in the taxi, but not before I counted my money and situated my keys for attack—with all the keys facing out between each finger in case I needed to swing at someone at a moment's notice. A girl could never be too careful.

Per the usual, I closed my eyes on the way home, not quite allowing sleep to overtake me. When the car came to a stop, I saw a white BMW double-parked outside my building.

Darrell? He came to my house? I smiled and immediately felt butterflies.

Turning to my driver, I thanked him for his service, handed him the money from my right-hand, and exited on the street side.

In front of my building—at the bus stop—Darrell was leaning on the hood of his car looking sexy as hell.

"I told you I'd see you later, didn't I…? I just wanted to make sure you made it home okay. You hungry?"

I was *soooo* tired from interning all day and dancing all night, and I had to be up early for a meeting the following day…but fuck it! We were here now.

"…I could eat," I said as dry as possible.

Darrell opened the passenger-side door for me, and I got in. We turned on 145th going east toward the Riverfront and found a spot overlooking the water. I still had an attitude, and he knew it. But my heart was beating out of my chest—we had never been alone together before…*ever*.

He pulled out a bacon, egg, and cheese with tomato from the corner store.

"H-How'd you know this was my favorite sandwich?" I asked, pleasantly surprised.

"You mentioned it once a few weeks ago. I was hoping you would come straight home because it was getting cold."

"How'd you beat me home *and* get a sandwich?"

"Don't worry 'bout all that," he chuckled. "Did you have a good night?"

"Yes. The only issue is that this guy I have a crush on didn't pay me any attention…and I had an attitude until he surprised me at my house and brought me my favorite sandwich. That was thoughtful *and* sweet."

Darrell laughed his deep quiet laugh, and my stomach fluttered.

"Well, I'm glad," he said. "We had those fights earlier, and I had to have my eyes on the floor and the monitors. I didn't think you cared that much to be honest, especially since you were getting money hand-over-fist tonight."

"*Hmm,*" I replied, and by then I had eaten half of my sandwich and wrapped up the rest.

My mind was moving fast. I had no desire to waste time talking.

"Do you wanna come up to my place so we can talk without this console between us?"

Darrell thought a lot longer than I thought he should have.

"Yes, I do…but I can't tonight. I have to get my daughter ready for school in the morning."

He could tell I was disappointed.

"But I promise you, I will take you up on that offer very soon…and as you can tell, I always keep my promises."

Irritated, I started texting G. Money before Darrell could pull out of the parking lot.

Today 3:08 AM

Me: Hey, G, you up?

G. Money: ...

Those dots meant that he was up, and I was about to get my back blown out!

Three

I was getting dicked down weekly by this hood booger named G. Money. I recognized that lying down with a guy named "G. Money" was problematic, and no, I don't know his real name.

He saw me walking toward the bus stop one day, pulled over in his Mercedes, and wrote his number down on a $100 bill. He said I had an ass that wasn't "built in New York" (true) and a smile that could "keep the city lit" (free game).

G. Money was the color of red clay dirt with an easy, wide smile. He smiled like he knew the meaning of life and wanted to share it with you. He was about 5'10 (in Timbs), with clear, bright, brown sparkling eyes. I found out later that his parents were from Ghana, which explained his untraditional good looks and beautiful white teeth. They were charmingly crooked in all the right places. He looked like if he had lived in the South, he would have played linebacker in high school. He was "thicka denna snicka" and had the kind of belly you wanna rub up against when the weather gets chilly, you know?

On our first date, he took me to the Russian Tea Room and ordered the salmon (pronounced with a hard 'l'), then wanted a bottle of their "best house wine," which made it obvious to me that he wasn't familiar with nice restaurants or proper etiquette. That was fine though because he was a cool guy who wanted to go out and have a good time. I honestly wasn't looking for more than that anyway.

Our conversation consisted of his cash, cars, kids, and goals for the block. He had made his money selling drugs and wanted to invest in real estate in Harlem before gentrification took hold. He went on and on about how land was one of the few commodities in limited supply and the role real estate plays in the eventual economic freedom of disenfranchised people. All the knowledge he had about the community along with his desire to become a social activist turned me on so much.

He told me he wanted to keep the power in the hands of the people. And that level of social consciousness is why I let him eat my pussy in the back of his Benz on our first date. (Don't judge me. Judge your mama!) But it was…trash.

There were copious amounts of dry tongue, finger stabbing, and tongue jabbing. *(Sigh.)*

I grabbed his dick through his joggers before we pulled over. (Yes, he wore joggers on a first date). And it was a *monster!* So, I figured I could endure this terrible head for greater treasures later.

Chiiiile, the head was so bad I had to tell him that I wasn't "feeling well" and to please drop me off. His jabbing made me sore, and I'm pretty sure his fingers weren't clean because I got a nasty yeast infection after that. *(Ugh!)*

After using some over-the-counter stuff and eating excessive amounts of yogurt, I was right as rain in a few days. About a week later, I received an unsolicited dick pic with the caption: *Ya' pussy juices still on my beard...wassup?*

I ignored the first two pics, but that third one came with some rice and peas attached, so I let him upstairs with the prerequisite of him bringing some food with him. And, bayyyy*beh*...dick was too bomb! I made sure he washed his hands thoroughly (scrubbing underneath his nails and clipping them) before he ever touched me again. His mouth game never improved, but the dick was outta this world. He fucked me like he had no job and had stored up energy just to pleasure me. He was a W.O.T.—a waste of time; someone to hang out with until something better came along. In my mind, this was an even exchange with no strings attached. Honestly, G. Money was just a lot of fun with no stress.

He answered my text right away—it was like he was *always* awake.

Today 3:09 AM

G. Money: Come through.

Me: See you in 5.

Once we pulled back up to my building, I started gathering my things.

"...so, see you soon, Nik?" Darrell asked.

"Maybe...I don't know," I mumbled. "I'm tired of the games, so...see you at work, I guess."

As I walked inside, I noticed G. Money standing at the front door. He let me in with a stank face.

"You was just in that nigga's car?"

I failed to mention that G. Money and I lived in the same building, so booty calls were a piece of cake. It also made leaving/coming home from dates a bit tricky, but he knew what it was.

He squinted, looking at the car, mumbling, "Dirtbag" under his breath as he let me in the building.

"Excuse me?"

He repeated himself, "You was just in that nigga's car?"

"Yeah, he's the club manager at Dream. He just gave me a ride home."

"Hmm." He was getting upset, so I ran over and hugged him from behind.

"G," I purred in his ear.

"...what? I swear, you a bird, man. You only text me late at night and never respond when I want some. It's always on *your* schedule. Then, you pull up from dates with big time drug dealers..."

"Whoa, whoa, whoa," I started. "First of all, Darrell is *not* a drug dealer. Like I said, he manages the club I work at. Secondly," I started purring in his ear from behind, "stop trippin'. I'm here with *you* right now. Now, let me up, so I can get some of that Ghanaian dick. When you hit me back on text, I started dripping...see?"

I grabbed his hand and stuffed it down my pants, *over* my panties. There was no way that I was gonna let him touch my pussy without witnessing a *thorough* hand-washing first.

The moisture I had from Darrell was very noticeable, making G. Money smile. He brought his finger to his mouth and tasted it.

"Damn, girl...if I did all that to you with just a *text,* wait till you see what I'm 'bouta put on you!"

Hurrying upstairs, I had to keep checking the time because I had a work meeting in the morning that I needed to prepare for. G. Money spotted me checking my watch.

"Hey, girl, don't be checking the time. I'll walk you home when I'm done with you."

I laughed because I knew it was about to go down like it always did.

Once we got inside his studio apartment, G. Money leaned all 210 lbs. of his body against mine, and I felt that monster against my stomach. It's like as soon as he got me inside the door, all the blood rushed to his dick, and I was very pleased. His breath smelled like stale weed and Remy as he kissed me hungrily.

His wet lips continued to explore mine, as he sucked my bottom lip and traced the outline with his tongue.

Maybe, him giving me some head won't be so bad after all, I thought.

I told him to go wash-up and meet me on his bed, which was literally just a mattress on the floor surrounded by Nike boxes. I already knew that was Fuck Nigga Characteristic #7, but I had already had sex with him at my house before I saw his place. *(shrug)*

G. Money came back from the bathroom smelling like Zest without any clothes on, and his body was beautiful…especially in the candlelight. I told you, he was built like a linebacker—solid and thick. He laid down on top of me grinding his dick against me, taking off my clothes, grabbing everything like he was going to die if he didn't get it.

He stopped when he got me naked and just admired my body.

"*Gooootdamn,* girl, your body is…let me just look at you for a minute. I like when you come over after work," he said, grabbing my breasts with his mouth. "You taste salty, and I love Lawry's."

I laughed at his corny ass—mostly because I wanted some of that dick tonight.

Kneeling beside me, he propped up my head and chest with one hand while he licked my left breast. Saving the right one for last was his thing—it was pierced, and he knew it would drive me *crazy* when he would tease the bar with his tongue, lightly flicking it before he would put my nipple in his mouth and then devour as much of it as he could. He was driving me crazy, and he knew it.

I couldn't understand how somebody so good at everything else could be so awful at giving head, so I decided to try again.

"G, she wants some of that same attention," I motioned toward my clit. And he graciously obliged, diving in with the same vigor he had on our first night together…but unfortunately, he just…couldn't get it right.

I mean, here was this fine specimen of masculinity making my body feel amazing in every other way, but when he got down to my pussy, he had no idea what he was doing. *(Sigh.)*

Beyond the tired tongue strokes and stabbing movements, he had the nerve to talk shit while he was down there too.

"Oh, yeah, you like that, don't 'chu? You're so nasty…yeah, baby, I feel you getting wet for me. You been waiting for this head all day, haven't you? You fuckin' bitch…oh, yeahhh."

I rolled my eyes.

"Oh, hell no! I ain't no 'fuckin' bitch,' G." I sat up quickly, grateful to be done with his finger jabbing.

"C'mon, you know I ain't mean it like that. I just thought you liked when I talk dirty to you…my bad," he said, grabbing my breasts and climbing on top of me.

I stopped him.

"Umm, where the condoms?"

"Oh, we still gotta deal with those? I mean, I'm safe, you know…"

I looked at him like he had three heads.

"Nigga, WHERE ARE THE CONDOMS? The fuck?"

I was about to just get up and go home between the terrible head and him acting like he didn't want to put one on. I was always wary of dudes who had no concern about condom usage. I was F-R-E-E, STD free—and planned to stay that way.

"…I ran out," he said, his dick softening by the moment.

"You'd better run out to the corner store and get some more," I said, aggressively.

After a moment's pause, I stopped him from getting dressed because he knew I was leaving. When he got my text, he didn't think to get condoms from the corner store just twenty-feet away? That was some dumb shit, and I immediately didn't have time for it.

"…you know what? Never mind. I'm out."

I started putting my clothes on and heard him fake looking through his drawers, tossing things over his head, searching for a condom like a cartoon character or something. It was honestly hilarious, but I was headed out the door anyway, so I just told him I'd catch him another time.

After grabbing my clothes quickly, I headed home. I took a shower and started to put my money up for the night into my secret stash, but all I saw was $20. My first thought was that I dropped it at G. Money's house, so I called him—this was too serious for a text.

"Don't try to get some of this dick now that you grabbed a condom or two from your house, Nikki. You stormed out of here like I disrespected you or something, damn."

"G, I don't have time for your emotions right now. Can you check to see if I dropped some money at your house? A couple hundred dollars?"

I heard him rummaging around, but I knew it wasn't there. At that moment, I realized I had given the taxi driver the wrong amount when I got out of the car.

FUCK!

Instead of giving him the $20 I had set aside to get home, I had given him the $800 I had earned that night. I wanted to cry. This was the shittiest night *ever*. No attention *or* dick from Darrell, G. Money tried to play me, and I was out almost a thousand dollars. Throw the whole day away! It was time to go to sleep and start over.

Four

I was up early the following day for my internship with Bel—*the* British fashion powerhouse to land on American soil at breakneck speed. Due to their success overseas and online, they just opened a New York flagship location in SoHo two-years ago, and people were clamoring for a chance to work *for* and *with* them. The store was on the ground-floor, and the offices sat right above, taking up several floors.

The sales department on the ground floor was very minimal—just neutral colors and very cold—but the offices upstairs were decorated with dark wood, warm jewel tones, and plants everywhere.

Walking into the office in the morning always made me happy because of the smile-inducing colors that were everywhere. All the fashion magazines were climbing over themselves to see what the elusive Todd Jones had done to his first American property—but he made it very clear (via press release) that he wanted to "protect the spaces where we work." He believed the places we choose to spend the majority of our waking hours should "belong more to the employees than the fashion world." I mean…how dope is that?

There was a rumor that Todd Jones would be coming to our location for an extended visit, but as lowly interns, we were often the last to know things of that magnitude.

My boss Emily was cool, but I didn't know if *she* knew who Todd Jones even was. Very few people outside of the world of fashion knew what he looked like; he never gave interviews and sent his assistants to all the fashion shows in his place to stream for him to watch.

The reclusive behavior of the CEO was part of what fueled the excitement around Bel—people wanted to know who he was. By working at Bel, I thought I would've caught a glimpse of him through our intranet or our email system since we all have to take photos for our email signature, but the messages he sent out to the company never showed his photo.

Due to how amazing and conscious the brand was, there must've been hundreds of applications every year, so I was extremely lucky to have secured this internship. My letters of recommendation were good, and I interviewed well, so they chose me and nine other lucky college grads to do all their grunt work and get an inside look at how Bel was run.

I wasn't sure if upper management really knew what they wanted in an intern, as the job description was confusing and contradictory to say the least. But they knew people would apply to work here if the job description was blank, so I don't think they really tried.

Most of this internship consisted of answering phones, providing administrative support, and running errands—if you weren't hustling like me. The reason I, a girl from "middle of the map, America," applied for this job was because I want to see all standards of beauty represented in fashion, and I knew the best way to change the system was from the inside, out.

Unlike many of my fellow interns, I asked to attend meetings I had *no* business attending, always volunteering to take minutes. That's how I found out the company gossip.

I set-up coffees with middle managers and asked them how they got into the business. I made them think they were more important than they really were, since most of them used to be interns just like two-years ago. I usually came in with the front desk staff and covered their lunches when someone was out sick. That was how I learned all the names of the head honchos.

One time, I covered the front desk completely, and Jasmine (the woman who had been there the longest) insisted that Kelly give me a day's pay from her paycheck because I did the job "so well." I've even offered to take out trash and clean-up after the models—they come midday and leave before our cleaning staff arrives, so unless someone offers to, the room will stay dirty until we are all gone for the day. Needless to say, dealing with models was my least favorite part—many of them were so entitled due to their looks, they thought the world (including unpaid interns) owed them something.

This morning, I lucked out and got to do the coffee run instead of fitting the models. Most of us interns had been designing our own clothes for years, so fittings weren't really fun anymore. But coffee runs meant you could keep "busy" and sit in the actual meetings instead of going crazy dealing with grumpy, hungry, models. Doing coffee runs meant there was a possibility that an intern could actually provide input. The higher-ups rarely asked us to speak, but if there was an opportunity to, it would be during this weekly meeting.

When I first started, one of the designers sent a model out in this awful Scottish pleated skirt, looking like a disaster, and everyone turned their nose up at how everything looked together. They asked Georgina (who had graduated college two-years ago, but whose father was owed a favor by one of the executives) what she thought of it. She gave her honest opinion, and they laughed at her…and not in a nice way. Once our boss informed her—and the rest of the room—that the skirt was a vintage piece made by the *one* and *only* Rustic House and cost more than her father made in a month, they laughed her out of the room…and she was never asked to get coffee again. In fact, I doubted she'd even stay in the world of fashion.

Suffice to say, getting the coffee came with its own set of landmines, but it was the only way to really get noticed by everyone at once. If an intern was asked their opinion, it wasn't because they really wanted it. They really just wanted to laugh at your ignorance. A lot of this world was similar to the strip club—people wanted to hear what they already thought. They didn't want to be challenged because they thought they've done the work already, came to their conclusion, and you just had to roll with it…unless you're smart, which if you haven't noticed, I happened to be.

Challenging someone's biases was a tricky thing to do if you wanted to remain in their good graces, but I was always up for a challenge.

We were on our fifteenth look of the day, and Karen from the panel asked me what I thought.

Smiling, I stepped forward.

"May I feel the material?"

When everyone nodded, I felt the skirt.

"…it's obvious to me that this is not material made in America…or this century, honestly. The way the fibers lay and the way the skirt is cut…*hmm,* this is from the house of Mi Chiamo—vintage, but this blouse is deceptively simple. Imani, can you walk away from me again, please…? See, it's cut small for a woman, but still androgynous…is this blouse—surely not—is this from Forever 21?"

The panel laughed and started clapping.

"Not even I spotted that mix of high and low," my boss said, quietly. "Well done, [*redacted*]. May I have another latte, please? Extra foam, double whip."

I NAILED IT! Today was gonna be a good day.

Successfully managing my internship and making a good impression every day was the only way I would be offered a position here in a few weeks. My internship was ending soon, and I knew having experience with Bel would look good on an application anywhere. Unfortunately, I didn't have any New York connections and no one I knew was in the world of fashion, so I was relying on my own achievements out here—unlike some of my peers. For me, working here would be "living the dream." I was just working to make enough money at night to afford life in Harlem until Bel hired me permanently…I was hoping to hear something soon.

*****

I raced home to take a short nap before work, and there was an envelope slid underneath my door. Six condoms were inside with sloppy handwriting on the front: *Do-over at your place? Text me.*

I texted G. Money laughing emojis before throwing the condoms in the trash. I always got a weird vibe from him—like he was trying to trap me by poking holes in the condoms or something. I planned to chill out on him for a while.

Today 7:09 PM

G. Money: I see you got my note.

Me: Yes, thank you. Lol.

G. Money: What time you want me to make it up to you?

In my head, I was thinking, *No time in the near future.*

Me: I have to work tonight, so I'll text you, okay?

G. Money: I never met a woman who works more than me. That's crazy, but I understand. Hit me up when you can.

Me: K.

G. Money: Hit me up, man—don't play!

Me: Okay! Lol.

Five

"Next stop, 145th Street!"

The subway announcer was clear for once, so I shook myself awake. I was daydreaming and had drifted off.

Darrell was on my brain heavy, and I didn't even have his phone number. I mean, what kind of man fondles a woman at a diner and then drops her off with no regard, no contact…no nothing? He was driving me crazy, mostly because I couldn't figure him out.

Most guys usually disclosed everything they wanted from jump—either in action or words. Initially, at least, they wanted attention, to be spoken to like they had the biggest dick in the room, sex, and food.

As relationships progress, you find the nuance into what they want and/or need. At first, it's pretty easy, but Darrell was anything but easy.

He was always respectful and kind to everyone at the club. Many people who decide to work in a strip club don't come from the most nurturing of backgrounds. Needless to say, they aren't spoken to with respect on a regular basis, so a man with power showing respect made him well liked by everyone.

Darrell never presented himself like a sleazeball. If he offered something, it wasn't because he was expecting anything in return, unlike plenty of other managers

I'd worked with before. Being a seemingly upstanding—and obviously, highly sexual—man made my body throb for him, but my mind experienced a way bigger attraction. He was a bit of an enigma; I couldn't figure him out, except now, at least, I know he was feeling me—*that* I knew for sure.

I wondered if he had ever been with any of the other dancers like he'd been with me, or if any of the other dancers lusted for him like I did. I had never heard them talk about wanting to do nasty things with him like they did other members of the staff who often offered them car rides home, gifts, even money, in exchange for sexual favors. Everything Darrell did was simply because he wanted to do it, with no expectation of a returned favor. That left me confused though, especially coming from the strip club world.

*****

"Do you like theater?" Darrell walked up behind me at the club and bent down to talk in my ear.

"Excuse me?" I said, twisting my body around to partially face him.

He sat down in one of the open chairs near me. There were plenty free, as it was another slow night.

"Have you seen *Fences* on Broadway yet?"

"No. I tried to get rush tickets a few times, but my number never got called. How did you know I would like theater?" I was perplexed.

"You seem like the type," he shrugged. "I have an extra ticket. Do you know anyone who could go tomorrow night?"

Hmmm, I thought. *Is he asking me out, or just giving me a ticket?*

He was so sexy that it was hard to focus on the question he was asking, but I managed to answer.

"*Me!* Me! I can go! But are you asking me to go with you, or are you just trying to give me a ticket?"

He hesitated before reciting Rule #8: *"Don't date any of the Dream staff—if you are discovered dating, one of you will be forced to resign...* I'm only offering you a ticket," he said with a mischievous look in his eye.

"Well, I will take you up on that offer then, *friend.* What time does the show start? And what are you planning to wear?" My mind started churning like crazy.

How am I going to get outta working tomorrow night? Do I have anything to wear? Will I have to go straight from my internship to the theater? Are we definitely fucking tomorrow?! But what if he really does just want to be friends? The way he looks at me, he definitely wants more than a damn friendship...right?

My brain was going a mile a minute.

"What am I wearing?" He let out an uncharacteristically loud laugh. "Women are crazy! I have no idea what I'm wearing. Look, what's your number? I'ma text you. We'll figure out what time to meet that way...I see some customers coming in now. I'll catch you later."

"Okay," I said, calmly, but inside, I was screaming like I was in 7th grade, passing notes again.

I GOT HIS NUMBER?! OMG!

The remainder of the night was blurring by. Darrell left soon after we spoke, and Hyro took over manager duties. It's safe to say that at the end of my shift, I floated all the way home.

*****

The following day, I ran out to Necessary Clothing on my lunch break to find the perfect outfit within my price range, which was difficult. My waist-to-ass ratio was crazy, so cheap spandex tended to "fit" all my curves, but made me look slutty.

Lycra worked with less "slut appeal," but it could be tricky once I pulled something up over my ass. Nonetheless, it was important for me to look classy without spending all the money I *didn't* have.

After only fifteen-minutes of searching, I spotted an outfit on a mannequin that looked perfect for me. A V-neck, light pink pantsuit with a thin red belt ended up fitting me like a glove, and my push-up bra gave me cleavage for days.

Looking at myself in the mirror, I turned around and approved with a big smile. I left the dressing room to check out my reflection in the big mirror, and everyone in the vicinity approved as well.

I heard a few comments like, "Yes, bitch!"

"Okay, girl, you must have a hot date tonight."

"*Oooh,* that pink and red looks fire on you!"

I was confident that I could step out, ready to razzle and dazzle Darrell.

After I was done, I nearly flew back to my desk, giddy and breathless, to finish my work, so I could get dressed and leave on time.

Darrell and I sent texts back-and-forth literally all day. I couldn't believe that he was just as funny, smart, and charming via text as he was in-person. He appeared to be the total package, and I couldn't wait to see him…and, hopefully, end the night with him inside me.

At the end of the day, I went to the restroom to get ready. Once I walked out, my co-workers started howling and making silly catcalls. They wished me well and helped me put on my coat before I left. They had no idea that my date was with the manager of the strip club where

I danced—and it had been hell trying to keep that from people I saw every day.

The show started at 8 p.m., so Darrell and I agreed to meet at Cort Theatre at 7:30 p.m. Since I was coming from work, it only made sense to meet there, especially since parking was *bananas* in Times Square.

I thought I would arrive before Darrell, but he was already at the box office when I got there, paying for the tickets with a little brown bag in his hand. Once he saw me, he walked over like he had a big dick and the whole world would wait for him to unleash it if he wanted.

We hugged before he pulled me away, looking me up and down.

"Wow! You look amazing. Damn, girl, I never thought you'd look just as good inside your clothes as you do at work."

I blushed.

"Thanks, Darrell…but, hey! I thought you already had tickets. What were you paying for at the box office?"

He shook his head.

"No, that was just will-call. The tickets were waiting for us here."

Even though I had used will-call before, my nervousness made me feel so dumb. And in that moment, I realized that Darrell was *completely* out of my league.

"I knew that. I guess, I'm just nervous," I looked down.

Grabbing my hand, Darrell looked me in the eye and said, "It's okay. I got you."

When I glanced up at him, I was grateful that I had worn panties because I felt tingles in my pussy I'd never had before.

"Hey, I got you something. I hope it fits. Let's walk in, and you can stop by the restroom and try it on."

My curiosity was piqued.

He bought me something? Is this a date? I was so confused.

Darrell led me over to the side to allow everyone to get to their seats, and...*mmmm,* he smelled good.

"What is that you have on? It smells amazing."

"I'll tell you later," he whispered in my ear. "Put these on and be sure to have it on correctly. Here's your ticket...I'll see you in there." He handed me a bag before grazing my cheek with his lips. His aftershave and stubble pricked my skin in the best way possible.

I walked as quickly as I could to the restroom, but there was a line four-ladies long.

FUCK!

Looking at my watch, I wasn't sure if I would be able to make show time with a wait this long.

Murmuring, I said, "God, forgive me" before I started walking with a limp over to the attendant and asked for the accessible restroom.

She looked at me suspiciously and pointed down the hall.

The restroom was so beautiful with exposed pipes and gorgeous antique wallpaper. I hobbled into the stall in case she was still looking and locked the door. I took a deep breath and opened the bag.

Inside was a pair of white, lace underwear and a little black bullet-sized device. My phone buzzed in my hand.

Darrell: [Redacted], put those panties on; put the bullet in the little pocket inside and hurry to your seat—left orchestra box.

Darrell: Just throw your old underwear away. I'll buy you some new ones.

I carefully unfastened my belt and pantsuit, making sure that I didn't get any deodorant on it or step on the fabric. I pulled down my multicolored cotton bikini-cut panties and smelled them. (Oh, you don't smell your own underwear? Everybody does it!)

There was no way I was throwing away these panties. They were Victoria's Secret, and that was at the *top* of my budget. Hell, I might wear them tomorrow since I *just-just* put them on before I came down here.

Not thinking twice, I stuffed them inside my bra, got dressed, and quickly hobbled back out of the restroom to my seat.

I had been to plays before in college, but never in a theater like this and certainly never in box seats. I felt like Julia Roberts in *Pretty Woman.*

Darrell and I shared the box with four other people I assumed were together. Darrell introduced me to them one by one. When I turned to my chair before sitting down, I kissed his cheek. He looked at me bewildered.

"I thought I told you to throw your panties away?"

The surprise must have shown on my face.

How could he possibly have known that I kept them?

Darrell leaned toward my chair and whispered, "That night with you at the diner…I didn't wash my hand for hours, so I could inhale your essence every time I moved. I know exactly what you smell like, and I know you're delectable…where'd you put them? In your bra…?"

I nodded silently, feeling exposed and turned-on all at the same time. My pussy was throbbing in a new way!

He put his hand on the small of my back and inched closer, revealing a small controller.

“This is the remote control for the vibrations you’re currently feeling.”

I stifled a squeal, as he slowly increased the sensation.

Nibbling my ear lobe, he said, “This is gonna be a good night.”

The bells chimed and the lights dimmed, indicating that it was time to begin. I was so turned on and nervous that I could barely concentrate on August Wilson’s most performed work. Thankfully, Darrell turned it off as the play began. I didn’t get much of a reprieve, however.

I had actually read this play before, so, gratefully, I knew the plot.

By the end of the first act, I was gripping the railing so hard I thought I was going to break it. Darrell would take me to the verge of orgasm and then pull back. It was torture, pure torture. When everyone stood up to clap, I had to remain seated because a wave of pleasure had come over me, I wasn’t even sure I could stand. The others in the box gave me the stink-eye, but what could I do during the beginning of an orgasm?

Turning toward him, I noticed Darrell was definitely aroused by this entire scenario.

At intermission, once our box was emptied of occupants, I leaned back, speaking to Darrell between gritted teeth.

“I cannot sit through another forty-five-minutes of this. I’m going to go take this-contraption off whether you approve or not. Hell, I don’t even care if my pants are wet!”

He chuckled.

“I understand. I thought you could take it, but I guess not,” he joked.

"No, I can take it. I just-I just can't here on Broadway. You're *literally* torturing me. I can't even enjoy the play."

"Haven't you read it already?"

At this point, our box was now empty, and I could speak at a volume that was above a terse whisper.

"That's not the point, Darrell." I started moving my hands wildly. "You can't just expect me to…"

He lightly grabbed my throat from behind. Thank God, our seats were in the back of the box in the shadows.

Then, he gripped my hip and started sliding his hand closer to my knee.

"Can't expect you to what…?"

Breathing hard, I grabbed his hand which was making its way between my legs.

"I can't expect you to what, [*redacted*]? *Hmmm?*" He licked the part of my neck that was exposed, humming in my ear as he flicked the vibrator back on. "My god, I wanna be inside you right now." He was talking in my ear and flicking my neck with his tongue. I could feel the pressure rising as he increased his grip around my neck.

"Open your eyes and look at all the people below us who have no idea you're about to cum in my hand."

He turned the vibrator up a notch and rubbed the entrance of my pussy; grinding on his hand was something my body did without my control at this point.

Nibbling at my ear he said, "Open your fucking eyes and cum for me right now."

At this point, anyone who was looking at us would know exactly what was going on, but I didn't give a damn.

I made eye contact with a beautiful older woman in the box across from us. She had silver locs down her back with a low-cut black dress on and seemed to be alone with a cocktail in-hand. She was looking at her program at first, but she must've felt me looking her way and looked up. First, she glanced at us; then, she narrowed her eyes as if to say, *"Are they doing what I think they're doing?"*

Her eyes got big as saucers, but she didn't stop looking—maybe, she couldn't. Her gaze was bringing me closer to the edge of orgasm, and I thought for sure that she was going to alert someone because she stood up exhibiting a gorgeous body before turning around to walk out. I slightly turned to alert Darrell to stop, but as quickly as I could blink, the woman walked in and closed the curtain behind herself.

Caressing her chest, she reached into her dress and carefully, thoughtfully, *lustfully* began rubbing her beautiful breasts right across from me. Turning around to make sure no one was coming, she hiked her dress up and started playing with herself—with one foot on the ledge of the box.

I couldn't believe my eyes, and I wondered if Darrell was seeing what I was seeing.

I continued grinding against his hand and feeling the vibrations, but I couldn't take my eyes off her. I wanted to cum with this beautiful stranger so badly.

When her breasts came completely out of her dress, and her eyes rolled back in her head, I lost it. I came so hard I had to bite my hand to keep from screaming. I was shivering with my eyes closed, riding the wave.

When I opened them and looked back, it was as if nothing had ever happened. *Did I imagine that?* The only evidence proving I was in reality was her breasts nearly spilling out of her dress as she sipped her drink and looked at her program once back in her seat.

Her companion came back seconds later and kissed her deeply.

Suddenly, the sound of Darrell's voice brought me back to reality.

"Damn, you're soaking wet." He released his grip on my throat. "Here, take my jacket…let's go to the restroom. You had to have soaked through your pants. Good thing you kept your panties after all, huh?"

I was so confused, turned-on, and angry that I could barely move. Darrell was standing with his jacket off, ready to throw it over my shoulders. A small puddle had formed underneath me, and his eyes got wide.

"I-I apologize; I took it too far. Damn, girl, can you even get up? I shouldn't have let you do that here."

I was so embarrassed that I didn't have words.

Darrell slipped the jacket over my shoulders, as we walked toward the restroom. Don't ask me why I still felt the need to do the fake hobble from earlier to the accessible restroom. I was going so fast no one would have believed that I even had a disability in the first place.

I walked past the line and into the restroom, checking behind me to make sure Darrell was still there. I motioned for him to come with me inside. He ducked into the door of the individual restroom and sat all 6'2 of himself down in the antique chair.

Strangely enough, this entire thing didn't pique my interest in having sex with him. He turned me on like nobody ever had, but I was so embarrassed that I had likely ruined that chair. And then, I started wondering who all could have seen me. *How did he know I would even be down for something like this?* My anger built considering factors I hadn't yet considered before. *Was this entire fiasco just for him? Did he have people planted in the audience to watch this entire thing go down? Was this about me and my pleasure at all? Or him being able to control me?* Maybe, I was being neurotic, but I didn't know if he was getting off on pleasuring me or controlling me. It was too confusing.

After Darrell sat down with one hand on the top of his pants and a smirk on his face like he knew why I had invited him in, I quickly removed my pantsuit. I stepped out of the remote-control panties. I attempted to sop up whatever moisture I had down there with toilet paper, pulled the panties out of my bra, and put them back on. Despite the fact that I was moving efficiently without any type of sensuality, I could see that he was aroused.

Standing there in my bra and panties, I looked over at him seductively.

"You like my body, Darrell? Why haven't I ever given you a lap dance before?" I walked over to him and dropped down, so I was bouncing on the balls of my feet and nuzzling his crotch. His dick smelled good through his slacks.

He was moaning, and his body was definitely responding to my stimulus package.

I looked up at him smiling, "Oh, you *do* like my—"

I was interrupted by the chimes, indicating the start of the second half of the play. I hurriedly put my pantsuit back on (for the third time that day), stuffed the soaking wet panties in his mouth, and walked out of the restroom with his jacket still on.

"Fuck you, Darrell. You don't control me," I said to myself, as I walked into the cold evening air headed for the train.

Six

"Let me get this straight. You left *box seats*...to a Broadway show...*during intermission because* he got you *too* wet?!" Shaun asked.

"Well, when you put it *that* way, it does sound dumb as hell." I was cracking up lying across my bed, chatting on the phone like a high schooler.

Shaun had been my friend since we were 11-years-old. She was like a little sister with a splash of best friend and was the only one back home who actually knew what I did for money in New York. She accepted me as I was without question, and for that, I was grateful.

We had been through some crazy things together growing up. She *had* to be my friend forever; she knew where all my proverbial bodies were buried and vice versa.

"[*Redacted*], you are *trippinnnnnn*'. Why didn't you fuck him that night?"

"I was embarrassed and mad. I would've been an 'Isabad' anyway."

Shaun erupted in laughter.

"Bitch, I haven't thought of Isabad in years!"

"Isabad" was a nod to Rodney—this model-type we had both bedded back home with the last name "Screw". Rodney was *fine*—like, *fine*-fine. He was so charming and dripping with Big Dick Energy that panties just dropped at his feet. He was the kind of fine that could pull the baddest chicks of every demographic and social level. I mean, he fucked our gorgeous high school exchange Spanish teacher from Brazil by October, and we had only started school in early September—and he wasn't even in her class. When he was a freshman in college, he fucked his way to an 'A' in statistics. The professor's wife was so grateful for his attention that she went into her husband's computer and changed his grade, and he didn't even ask her to. By senior year at Roosevelt, the A-list singer performing for our homecoming (who shall remain nameless) was texting *him* her hotel address and room number before she even left the afterparty.

You would think somebody with that kind of practice would be an excellent lover, right? Well, we called him Rodney "Is A Bad" Screw aka "Isabad". Get it? Despite the BDE, he was working with complete mediocrity; girth, length, motion…there were no redeeming qualities in regard to sex. He was a good friend and a great human being—but an *aw*ful lover. The last time we had sex, we were a few days from graduation, and he was going down on me. Someone had thankfully given him lessons, so I came right in his mouth—twice.

He got up to put a condom on that tampon-sized penis of his, and I sobered up right away. It didn't matter because he was so drunk, he couldn't tell the difference between couch cushions and a vagina anyway. He got on top of me and gave that couch the business! I was so confused because he was moaning and groaning but was nowhere near my pussy. After about twelve strokes, he was done. The couch probably calls him "IsaBad" too.

Shaun slept with him a few times. It was just hard to believe somebody *that* fine and who'd had sex with *that* many women would be that awful. Shaun didn't think his member was small, but her issue was (also) the motion in his ocean. To circumvent the possible couch situation, she rode him, and, still, he just wasn't sure how to respond with his hands and pelvis. She said it was like riding a bull that wasn't plugged in. She kept trying to spur him into action but to no avail. He "ISBAD" Screw. Period.

"This is the guy you've been *dying* to have sex with; he makes you cum without even touching you, and you run off without even looking back?! You both have serious issues," she laughed. "Have you seen him at work? Has he texted you?" Shaun could not stop laughing.

"No. It's been four-days since #Broadwaygate, and it's been radio silence…Shaun, it's *not* funny!"

"'Hashtag Broadwaygate?'" She burst into laughter again. "did you say the word 'hashtag'?"

"Anyway," I rolled my eyes. "I wonder if he hasn't been at work because he's more embarrassed than I am."

Shaun changed her tone.

"*Oooh,* I didn't think about *him* being embarrassed. I just assumed he thought you would beat his ass." She started laughing again, but only because she knew I wasn't a fighter—not unless I was pushed into a corner. So, I wasn't beating anyone's ass, which made her statement that much more hilarious to us both.

"Why don't you just text him?" she asked, innocently.

"Because he will win. And I refuse to let him win! I control my body, not him," but as I said it, I knew it wasn't completely true. "The truth is, Shaun, I'm still insanely embarrassed. I squirted through my clothes for God's sake. How do you come back from that, to look someone in the face after something like that?"

Shaun was still laughing.

"How do you *cum* back?!"

"You know what? You're no help to me at…all. Goodbye. I have to go get ready for work…also, I hate you. So, there's that," I said, rolling off my bed and attempting to get ready for work.

"Well, I love you, so you can't get rid of me that easily. My final thoughts—no Jerry Springer—just text him. Tell him you felt disrespected or just that he was *trippin'*-trippin'. Or, shit, just tell him you wanna fuck. You have *always* played too many games."

"Maybe, I'll text him. I don't know yet. I don't wanna lose. I'm not gonna give-in. Hey, fuck him. Goodbye. I love you—I gotta go."

I put my phone in my back pocket and contemplated what I would say to Darrell via text. I had to be vulnerable, yet maintain my cool.

I felt my back pocket buzz and assumed Shaun had texted me something ridiculous, but it was a Cash App notification for $200 from a name I didn't recognize—*D. Bagggery*.

I opened the notification.,

D. Baggery: Sorry about your pantsuit, and for embarrassing you. Please, go buy another one… on me. See you later at work.

"Oh, shit!" This battle was officially over, and I won!

Jumping on the bed, I kicked my feet up in victory.

Seven

Friday morning, I found myself mentally preparing for a long day. I arrived at work at 8 a.m. and was given the responsibility of staying after-hours to greet our international guests at this swanky bar we had rented out for the night. This was definitely one of the coolest parts of my job—meeting people from all over the fashion world. Only a handful of people attended this meeting.

C-suite executives, high upper management, and six guests were flying in, but no other intern was asked to be in attendance. Being the "face" of the company for international guests was a big fucking deal! It meant they trusted me and were trying to confirm if others saw the same potential they did—at least that's how I felt about it.

Emily instructed me to take everyone's phones and lock them in a case, giving them half the key needed to retrieve them at the end of the evening. She said Todd Jones may have been making an appearance and preferred not to have any photos of him taken that he had not approved. It was a bit strange to me, but all the guests seemed to know about this rule and handed their phones over without issue.

I was poised at the entry in a cute little black dress and a pair of sensible yet cute heels, sipping on water with lime while I waited for our last guest to arrive. I saw Emily walking in my direction with a smile and a drink in-hand, one of the signature cocktails our mixologist Mich put together. She was this super thick woman with cute braces and a cool demeanor. I met her at a private sip-and-paint event when I was working as a semi-nude model. Apparently, the help she was supposed to have at that event bailed on her at the last minute, but she held it down without breaking a sweat.

When Emily asked us if we knew someone who could make cocktails and sign an NDA, I instantly thought of her, and luckily, she was available. She also had over 30k followers on social media, so she knew her stuff.

"[*Redacted*], have a sip of this; it's *sooo* good! What are you drinking?" Emily picked up my glass and smelled it. "*Water?!* Oh, no, that will not do. Everyone has noticed you working hard prepping for today, coming in early and staying late with no complaints...you deserve this drink!" she said, taking my water and pushing the tasty cocktail towards me.

"Emily, we still have one more person arriving," I laughed. "I didn't want to have a drink until they were all checked-in."

Emily was only a few years older than me, but it *felt* like she had already experienced the best that life had to offer. She was from Upper East Side New York and came from money—old enough that she inherited a rent-controlled apartment, but not *crazy* old because her grandparents had run themselves into early graves working toward creating a legacy.

"I'll hear nothing of the sort, [*redacted*]! You have been a phenomenal intern. You're apologetic for being on time or early, you have ultimate confidence in your ideas and know how to express them, and you are truly dependable. That last one is hard to find in this industry. This is a toast from me to you, so *salud!*"

I smiled as we clinked glasses.

"Emily, this is *delicious!* Mich was such a great choice for an important night like this one. And thank you for your appreciation. It feels good to be noticed for all my hard work." I took a deep breath before continuing. "And hopefully…we can discuss a more permanent situation in a few weeks?"

"You just read my mind, [*redacted*]." She clinked glasses with me again, and I exhaled a silent sigh of relief. "I also wanted to make sure that you are taking everyone's phones and locking them away, right?"

"Yes. No one has given me any trouble either. I think they're looking forward to being unreachable," I laughed.

"I don't even know why I asked. I knew we were in good hands with you." She raised her glass a final time before turning around to join the rest of the team inside.

I could barely contain my excitement as I went back to my post to wait for the last guest to arrive. In a matter of weeks, I could, maybe, possibly, hopefully, be offered a job at Bel.

This cannot be real! I thought.

Taking another sip of the tasty Chambord berry vodka cocktail, I looked up to see that our final guest had arrived.

He was dark as midnight with a gorgeous, shiny beard that connected immaculately. His hair was shaved on the sides, but the middle was dumb long. It was parted into an intricate cornrow pattern and pulled into a fair-sized bun. Even with it tied up, I could tell that he had hair a woman would love to run her fingers through.

I had only set my eyes on him for 3.5 seconds, and I could already tell that he was comfortable no matter where he was; his presence entered the room before he did.

The tan shirt he wore under his European-cut navy suit had the top button undone just enough that hints of a tribal tattoo peeked through. He radiated BDE—it was almost palpable, but I kept my composure. I *was* at work after all.

I reached out to shake his hand, and his were warm, masculine, and enveloped mine so easily. He wore two gold chains, a beautifully handcrafted ring, bracelets, and a wooden watch. He smelled like the woods after a rain—clean and fresh—despite just arriving from JFK. In a word, he was *beautiful.*

I felt blood rushing to my cheeks and my nipples hardening. I knew the only way to really capture his beauty was to see him naked, and he hadn't even spoken a word yet. I silently wondered how old he was since the darker the skin, the harder it was to pinpoint actual age.

"Welcome back to New York! Thierry Jorrington, I presume?"

"Yes, thank you for this warm reception. I hit a terrible snag at Heathrow, but luckily, they were able to get me on the next flight."

I thought, *Oh, shit, this nigga is from London. His accent...OH, MY GAWD!*

"Ah, you travelled from London. Are you from there?"

He removed his suit jacket to reveal a slim-thick man with deltoids, biceps, and triceps popping. Not to mention the way his shirt fit, it was clear that washboard abs lay underneath. Whoever he was, he took great pride in his appearance and clearly worked out.

"No, I'm originally from Rouen, France, but have called London home for quite some time now."

The twinkle in his eye shined brighter the longer he looked at me. They took me back to the last time I was on the ocean, and I was mesmerized.

"Je m'appelle, *[redacted],*" I said innocently, dusting off my French from my freshman year of college.

He grabbed my hand to check for a wedding ring.

"Mademoiselle, how are you doing tonight?"

"Tres Bien...now"

We both paused for a moment, my hand in his, until I snapped out of his spell.

This man sparked my attention, but as an intern on a *very* special assignment, staying in my lane was what I had to do.

"Can I offer you a drink, Thierry?"

"That would be amazing. Do you have any Evian?"

"The sparkling stuff is inside...not indulging in any spirits tonight?" I asked with a wink, as I handed him a Voss.

"Thank you. And, yes, I definitely plan to have a drink, later...*much* later tonight. You'll have to tell me about a few trendy places around my Airbnb, so I can wind down after these awful travel plans."

"Sure. What part of Midtown are you in?" I asked, enthusiastically.

He laughed.

"Do I look like a Midtown guy...?"

"Do you really want me to answer that?" I joked. "Actually, you look like you could fit in anywhere."

"Well, I'm staying in Harlem. I prefer it over anywhere else, so I can walk where James Baldwin walked."

Oh, my god, he knows the works of James Baldwin?!

I was looking at a Black-French-Brit unicorn. I was surprised that my panties hadn't melted off yet.

"Yeah," he continued. "My father is actually American. He came across the pond for work, met my mother, and never left Europe. So, I have quite a bit of American history…sorry, I don't know why I'm telling you this. You're just extremely easy to talk to, which is odd for me."

"Ah, T, there you are." Karen made sure to walk her hating-ass over, breaking up the moment. "I see you've met our *intern* [*redacted*]," she said with a fake smile.

"Yes, Karen, she is quite charming." He looked at me with lust in his eyes.

"…well, I have people I need to introduce you to. Please, come with me," she said with insincere warmth.

"Yes, I'll meet you over there shortly." Karen hovered around until Thierry turned and said, "Karen, we have forty-minutes before we need to begin our presentation. I'm sure I'll be able to meet everyone either before *or* after that."

"…but, Thierry," she started.

"I'll see you soon, Karen," he said sternly, interrupting her and turning back to face me. It felt so good to see Karen get put in her little raggedy place. I had to admit, I was impressed.

Karen turned around in a huff.

"No problem, T," and at that moment, I could tell she wanted him bad, and she was jealous of the attention he was giving me.

Karen was a head honcho at our company, and for some reason, she had it out for me. She was 50+ and still wore a size 4. She told us once that she prevented hunger by smoking cigarettes. Clearly, she had done it her entire life, and it showed all in her face and skin. Some of our visiting executives would make googly eyes at her, but she got no play from Thierry, and I was loving it!

I remember once she was giving the interns a presentation, and I raised my hand to correct one of her facts. She ranted and raved about how wrong I was, how I would never make it in this industry, how I needed to keep my big mouth shut...but she didn't realize Emily had snuck into the back of the room. Emily calmly interrupted her and prompted her to go to the next slide, which only proved that what I was saying was true. Karen's face got *soooo* red—it was *the best!*

Strangely enough, I knew everyone's title at this party, but not Thierry's. I couldn't find it in any of the emails either, so his level of importance to the company was still a mystery to me...but, clearly, Karen knew.

"So, what are we doing after this?" he asked.

I honestly was surprised by how forward he was. It must have shown in my face, because suddenly, he grabbed my hand.

"I thought we were on the same page, *non?*" As he switched between English and French, I felt myself breathing harder.

Now, deciding between going to work and hanging out wasn't difficult—Money. Over. Everything...mostly. But there was something about him that was giving me pause. I needed to buy some time.

"Just see me before you leave tonight. Go handle your business. *Au revoir.*"

"See you later," he said, as he walked over to join Karen.

This was a great evening with fabulous guests; we had DJ Big Brooklyn in the house spinning Chillhop, so everyone was in a good mood. When Thierry finally requested everyone's attention over to the big monitors on the screen, he thanked us all for joining him at Bel's New York location. The presentation was amazing. He spoke on the history of the company and expected financial and social trajectories.

He wanted to donate a percentage of every dollar earned to increase homeownership and small business ownership across underserved metro areas within the United States where gentrification had taken hold. I swelled with pride at being chosen to be a part of a company with such a conscious social footprint, and, honestly, the plans he laid out made my pussy throb with anticipation. I was pretty sure I was going to blow-off work and hang out with him, just because his vibe was *everything.*

While Thierry described working with different organizations in San Francisco, Detroit, and New York, my mind began to wander.

Why hadn't I ever seen his name on anything dealing with our corporate offices before? Is he a consultant? If not, what position does he hold? Why is he presenting this to everyone at the New York location?

I stood beside Mich, sipping my second drink of the night, and Thierry's presentation was reaching its close.

"That nigga got that…what do you always say?" Mich whispered.

I whispered back, "*Je ne sais quoi,*" as lusty thoughts continued to cross my mind.

"Yes, that's exactly it," she beamed, and we both tried to stifle our girlish giggles.

"I think I'm gonna try to fuck him tonight."

Mich gave me a silent high-five.

"*Biiiiitch*, you better! I bet it's good too. *Mmm, mmm, mmm,* that man is fine."

The last slide showed Thierry in a malasana yoga pose on the summit of a mountain. The name *T. Jones, Creator* was superimposed, and I almost spit out my drink. This was why no other interns were there and why we all had to lock up our phones upon arrival. The reclusive creator of Bel was not "Todd Jones," as was often publicized, but Thierry Jorrington! Consider my mind blown.

The creator, founder, and creative director of Bel wants to hang out with an intern from Missouri?

As the presentation ended, the room was buzzing with energy and excitement. After taking my drink to the head in one gulp, I headed to the restroom before running right into Thierry.

"*Soooooo,* we're hanging out tonight, right?" he asked, as he softly grabbed for my hand.

Overwhelmed, I began to stutter.

"You-You're technically my boss. Like, my boss' boss' boss..."

He frowned, pausing for a moment.

"Indeed. I didn't really consider that aspect of it. Listen, I don't want to make you feel uncomfortable or like you *have* to go out with me to keep your job or something. I mean, you were considering it before you knew who I was, right? Let's just pretend I'm not who I am and go have a round."

"Honestly, Todd, uh, Thierry…Boss," I mumbled. "I don't even know what to call you…"

"Call me 'Thierry.'" His dark eyes were dancing as he looked intently into mine.

"Thierry, I want nothing more than to go out with you tonight, and I'm not worried about losing my job. Your energy is palpable, and all the things you've done/plan to do for this world are…" I struggled to find the words.

"Amazing? Fantastic? Surprising?" he laughed, coming up with words that absolutely described his contribution to this world, as he took a sip of his drink.

"No. The word I was looking for was…'stimulating'."

Now, it was his turn to be flustered.

I smiled.

"Honestly, Mr. Jorrington—"

"Please, call me 'Thierry,' [*redacted*]. If you call me 'Mr. Jorrington,' I may have to treat you like an employee and *make* you do what I tell you…is that what you want?" He had a smile behind his eyes. "Plus, you were calling me 'Thierry' when you spoke beautiful French to me; why should that change now?"

"Okay, Thierry," I said, nervously. "Honestly, I had plans to go to work after this. I'm sure you know this internship is unpaid, so while I would really love to hang out with you, I do *need* to get to the club."

Inside, I hoped he would convince me not to go. But, rationally, I knew I needed to. Darrell was working tonight, and we really needed to talk.

Thierry glanced down at his watch.

"It's about 10 p.m. now…how much do you make this late bartending? You're a bartender, right?"

Without missing a beat, I lied, nodding vigorously, wishing I still had more liquid courage in my cup. There was really no need to correct him. What difference would it make?

Doing a few quick calculations in my head, I figured I could make about $400 tonight—$500, if it was really lit. The hustler in me tacked on a couple hundred dollars before presenting him with a number.

"I could make about $700, $800 if the club is bangin'," I responded with the most earnest face I could muster.

Thierry peeled off ten $100 bills and put them in my hand discreetly.

"For your time…what's the name of the club you bartend at anyway?"

"Well, damn!" I said, looking at the money in my hand and actively ignoring his question. "I have no reason not to go with you now."

I stalled on answering his question while I tried to make up a fake bar name, hoping he wouldn't suggest going there or look it up on his phone. All the while my head was on a swivel looking around for Karen, or anyone really, I didn't want anyone I worked with to see us speaking in such hushed tones like this.

"Thierry, let's talk about all that later, okay? And thank you. This is very kind of you. Let's hop in a cab on the corner of—"

"No," he laughed softly, interrupting me. "Meet *me* outside. I'm about to leave now. Don't worry. I'll make sure no one sees you with me."

"How can you leave? Everyone will be looking for you."

He unlocked his phone and smiled, scrolling through something.

"[*Redacted*], I run this company, remember? I leave when I want. And I want to leave with you—right now."

As an independent 20-something living in New York, I typically called all the shots in my life, especially when it came to dating. So, Thierry taking the lead in a calm yet strong way started a quiet storm in my panties. I felt myself throbbing in his direction as he made a call.

"Brandon? Yes, I have a gorgeous woman coming downstairs shortly. She's wearing a little black dress and strappy sandals. Yes…oh, and she's shaped like an Orangina bottle. Please, stand outside the car so she knows where to go. Thank you. See you soon." He then turned to me. "Can you be ready in thirty-minutes?"

Stuttering again, I answered quickly.

"I-I-I, yes. Yes, I can."

"Okay, you go out first. Brandon, my driver, is expecting you. You can't miss him," he said before walking off—and I went to speak to Emily.

"You're still here?" she said like she was disappointed in me. "Go, go, go! Aren't you supposed to be gone by now?"

It was like she was reading my mind.

"Thank you, Emily. What time do you want me here tomorrow?"

"Tomorrow is Saturday," she laughed. "I will see you on Monday…can you come in at 8 a.m., so we can prep for the meeting at 10 a.m.? I cannot tell you how helpful you have been tonight. Thank you! Also, put an appointment on my calendar for a week after our guests leave, okay? Don't let me forget!"

After receiving my tasks for next week, I ran to grab my things, but not before noticing that I had a notification.

Today 10:15 PM

Darrell: You comin' in tonight?

Darrell: We have a lot of new girls that don't know what they're doing. We need some vets in here.

This was the first I had heard from him since #Broadwaygate outside of his Cash App message.

I opened the text, left it on read, and ran outside.

A tall slender man with chiseled features in a chauffeur hat was waiting for me right outside as Thierry had mentioned.

"Hello. Guest for Mr. Jorrington?"

"Yes. Brandon?" I asked, breathlessly. I had damn-near jogged to get there.

"Yes, madam. You were exactly as he described. Please, follow me."

We walked over to a matte gray Jaguar XJ with tinted windows. It even had European plates. I had to stop for a minute and reflect.

Damn, this dude isn't rich...he's wealthy.

"Mr. Jorrington will be out soon."

Brandon opened the back door for me, and I slid inside. The interior was dark, and the tinted windows alongside the moonless night made it difficult to see at first. But the inside looked like an Apple store—all-white with clean lines.

"Brandon, can I use this charger?"

"Of course, madam; help yourself to whatever you see back there. Press that triangle right there, and the compartment will open. Take that out, and you'll see another compartment. In the first one is The Oracle—a high-end strain of marijuana that closely mirrors the effects of LSD and a bong cleaned out by hydropower after every use. Go deeper, and you'll see on the right is cocaine, the middle contains bottles of absinthe, and the left is Adderall. Should you desire anything else, please, let me know, and I'll procure it for you...oh, here comes Mr. Jorrington now."

What the entire fuck have I gotten myself into?

Brandon opened the other door, and Thierry removed his jacket before getting in. I got an even better look at his torso. He had unbuttoned one more button on the top, and I could see more of the chest-plate tattoo he adorned.

He got in and put his hand on my knee, leaning over and whispering in my ear.

"I have one question for you...are you hungry?"

That clean-forest-after-a-rain mixed with sandalwood smell was intoxicating.

"I could eat," I said in what I hoped was a strong voice.

"I see Brandon has given you the tour already—feel free to take whatever you'd like."

"Um, yes, he did…and, honestly, it's a bit overwhelming," I said, apologetically. "I don't really do drugs. Every now and then, I may take a hit of someone's joint, but nothing too much. I'm not really a drinker either, so absinthe sounds crazy. Is it the *real* absinthe that's outlawed in the States?"

"Indeed, it is."

"Thierry, hell no," I laughed. "Yo, you're crazy forreal."

"So, you don't want any of these? Nothing…?"

"I may have a glass of wine or something, but nah; this stuff is too much for me."

I must have looked terrified because he pulled me closer.

"You give off this 'down for anything' energy. I thought for sure you'd want something in my compartment. That's why I had Brandon show it to you. I don't do drugs either, except one." He pulled out a tab. "I love ecstasy when I'm at a club with a beautiful woman. Will you do one with me?"

Now, even though I didn't know this man from a can of paint, he did own the company I worked for, so he couldn't possibly have ill intentions for me, right?

"We'll see," I said, trying to stay light as possible.

"Oh, you hit me with the 'we'll see,' huh?" he laughed. "You're funny…we're going to have a great time." He patted my leg and looked in my eyes; they were striking. "I like you. You're quite different, you know?"

"…so, I've been told."

"Brandon, please, take us to Boku."

"Right away, sir."

I didn't realize the car was running until we pulled off because the engine was so quiet. We rode down the street laughing and talking until we arrived at our destination.

The Korean BBQ spot—Boku—was packed at 10:30 p.m. on a Friday, but somehow, we got a table right away. Thierry ordered for us both, and we spent the night cooking the food and laughing the entire time, making fun of Karen and other things about the industry. The more time we spent together the harder it was raining in my panties. The way he put his hand on the small of my back as we exited the building sent a chill up my spine, and resisting the strong desire to kiss him was becoming very difficult.

"Can we go somewhere else?" I asked, not wanting the night to be over just yet.

"*Ummm,*" Thierry hesitated, and I thought, maybe, I had overstepped my bounds. My face felt hot.

As he pulled out his phone, I said, "Oh, I'm sure you're tired from travelling. You can just take me home." I was trying to give him an out; apparently, I had misread the signs.

He was leaning on his car as he pulled me in close and kissed me lightly on the lips.

"This night isn't even close to being over, my dear. You may have sensed my hesitation because I'm not sure where to take you next."

We ended up at Beauty & Essex where popular Instagram influencer @AllThingsMikita was having an invite-only launch party for her new brand. We were in the Pearl Lounge, and the music and drinks were amazing; in fact, I think DJ Big Brooklyn was there too. He spotted me and waved, making the money sign with his hand—he was clearly hustling tonight.

After walking back from saying, "Hello," Thierry asked me into the restroom and brought out the ecstasy again.

"Will you take a trip with me?"

When I nodded, he took a pill, swallowed it with some Evian, put another on his tongue, and kissed me so quickly that I wasn't even sure that it had really happened. He pulled me close to him and instinctively, I opened my mouth to accept him. He had pillow soft lips, and he kissed me with passion and tenderness. I felt the pill transfer to my mouth, and he began to pull away. But I was enjoying this too much, so I sucked his bottom lip and bit it lightly before letting go. He looked at me with surprise. I swirled the pill around on my tongue before washing it down with a fancy drink. It was already midnight, and my night was just beginning.

Once the afrobeat set started with Fela Kuti, I damn-near ran out to the dance floor. I was really enjoying myself when a guy started to dance with me. He was keeping up with me too, which can be difficult. Guys usually are intimidated by my stamina and the size of my ass, but he clearly had moves of his own.

When I turned around, I saw that it was Usher! Like, *whhaaaaat?*

"Damn, lil' mama, you really got moves. What you doing after this?"

"I'm with him." I pointed at Thierry who was smiling, making his way over to us.

"Ush…"

"Thierry! Man, I didn't know this was you right here. My bad."

"No big deal, Ush, man; I was enjoying the show. Don't stop on my account."

There were a lot of rhythm-deficient people there, so I get why he was dancing with me. But the ecstasy was starting to kick in, and the feeling of him behind me with his hands on my waist felt *so* good. The spell was broken when some drunk partiers started trying to dance with us, stumbling and bumbling around the dance floor. I hugged Usher and thanked him for dancing with me; then, I went to look for Thierry.

He wasn't hard to find, as I felt his eyes on me the whole time. He was hugged up with this slender, *gorgeous,* Middle Eastern woman.

"Monika, this is [*redacted*]. She runs one of the biggest agencies in the tri-state area and is a good friend."

"Nice to meet you!" I held out my hand. When she took it, I couldn't help but notice how soft her skin was. "May I rub your hand, please?" I asked. She threw her head back, laughing. "Did you give this poor girl ecstasy?"

"Yes, yes, he did…and it feels *soooo* good."

She patted the seat beside her, indicating that I should sit. I was so glad I could sit down and continue to rub her hand because it was stimulating something inside me. It wasn't sexual per se—it just felt amazing.

She and Thierry continued their conversation, but I could only hear pieces of it now, as I was entering a different world.

My favorite rap song broke through this world of intense sensation I was floating in, and the urge to dance was stronger than continuing to feel how soft and amazing Monika's hand felt.

I jumped up and grabbed Thierry's hand.

"Come on, let's dance. I love this song!"

Apparently, everyone loved it too, because the entire room was up dancing and grinding on one another. Had everyone taken ecstasy too?

"Yes, let's all dance!" Monika said.

Monika and I were dancing face-to-face, and Thierry was behind me. It was like we were moving together, the three of us.

Monika put her hand around my waist.

"I love your hips and ass," she yelled over the music.

Thierry said, "Me too," and they started kissing right there with me in the middle of the dance floor. Feeling their bodies around me felt amazing, so I just leaned over and started kissing them too.

We were all making out when I felt Thierry behind me again. He was pressing against me so hard I could barely contain myself.

I broke away and turned around.

"Thierry, if you don't fuck me in the bathroom, I'm leaving."

"Monika, take care of my girl while I go take care of something, please." He got close to my ear. "I'm gonna rip your tights open when I get back."

Oh, shit! He is wild, and I was with it...but what did he need to go take care of?

Monika and I were still dancing, laughing, and having a great time when Thierry returned. He had a tough time making his way through the crowd, as literally everyone was out here sweating, dancing, just having a good time.

When he finally got to us, Monika gave me an amazing kiss goodbye.

"Watch out for this guy; he can change your life," she laughed. "Thierry, I love you. Have a great time tonight."

Once she was gone, Thierry began to dance with me, grinding on my ass like nobody's business. I was lowkey surprised that this Brit had this much rhythm. I felt him get hard against my ass, and the quiet storm inside me was building—it felt like a tsunami.

As I continued to become lost in the moment, suddenly, I could feel him pull away. When I turned around to see what was up, he had his entire dick out—with a condom on.

Sheesh.

It was *everything*—length, girth, *and* a condom? And the fact that he put a condom on before needing to be told turned me on even more.

I quickly turned back around so my ass was against him. And while I felt my dress raise up on account of us dancing, I think he was doing his part as well. Suddenly feeling my tights rip up the seam of my ass and my panties move to the side, Thierry lifted my booty cheek up, providing him with the opening he needed.

"Don't worry, I just washed my hands, and…my god, you are wet." He put his fingers in his mouth. "I can't wait to taste you later…"

As I looked around, no one was the wiser to what was happening. Meanwhile, I was damn-near crying from frustration because he only had the tip in. But just the tip stretched me out to the brink of pleasure and pain, and it was killing me with anticipation for what the entire dick was going to feel like swollen inside of me.

"Are you okay?" he asked.

"Fuck me, please," I managed to say.

"I can't very well *fuck* you…at least, not here. But I can give you a taste of what's to come."

He slowly and excruciatingly slid his dick inside me. I was 100% sure I gasped and that I was no longer dancing. He filled me all the way up and the way he just stood inside of me without moving was driving me crazy.

"Are you okay?" he asked again with a little mischief in his voice. "Or are you orgasming with your boss Mr. Jorrington?"

Since I couldn't respond, he just laughed in my ear.

"You're in for a good night then, aren't you, love?"

My eyes were closed, so I didn't notice anyone walking toward us until I heard Thierry's voice.

"Usher, pleasure seeing you again; we have to collab on my next project. I have something big coming, and I need you, okay?"

"Bet. Thierry, good to see you, man," he said, and they slapped hands. It was the same hand that had been inside of me. If I wasn't still cumming, I would have been mortified.

"Little mama, you're amazing. If you ever wanna dance in the studio, please, call my assistant. I'm always down to do some freestyling."

All I could do was nod and take his card.

Was Usher flirting with me while another man was inside of me? I mean, he didn't *know,* but still. It was too much!

"Let's get out of here" Thierry said, as he pulled out of me swiftly.

I couldn't help but shiver, feeling the emptiness he left from the fullness of his dick.

He pulled the back of my dress down and grabbed my things. Waving goodbye to his friends, he texted Brandon to pull the car around. Once we got inside, I could barely contain myself. This was *insane.* Nobody smells good, fucks good, treats you well, *and* is rich. Not a chance. Something had to be wrong with him.

"Brandon, can you take us to the brownstone, please?"

"Of course, Mr. Jorrington," he said, as we headed uptown.

*****

As I woke up the next morning, the last thing I remembered was stumbling up a few stairs in the semi-darkness, kissing Thierry, and feeling like I was drifting on a cloud. My mouth felt like it was made out of cotton balls, and I was super anxious, like I had missed something important. I looked around the room, and the sun was up. It was shining so brightly I thought it was already the afternoon. Surely, I hadn't slept the entire day away.

Sitting up quickly, I grabbed my phone, and it was only 8:45 a.m. I fell back into the billowy pillows, relieved that it wasn't noon yet, but frustrated that I was awake so damn early.

The natural light streaming through the windows gave the bedroom a beautiful glow. It was decorated in cool tones with a minimalist Swedish design, like an expensive version of IKEA. A little like our offices in SoHo—so it felt plush and cozy.

Beside me was Thierry knocked-out with his mouth wide open. He was shirtless, and I appreciated the view very much, as his skin was even more beautiful in the sunlight. The entire left-side of his shoulder and pecs were tattooed with beautifully intricate designs and vibrant colors. It was truly art.

Peeking underneath the covers, I noticed that I had on all my clothes from the night before.

Did we not have sex? We had that dance floor adventure, but was that it?

I got up to rinse my mouth out and do the wash rag/toothbrush thing, so my breath didn't smell like death warmed over.

Since it was still so early and I had nowhere to be, I decided to try to wake up Thierry for some morning head. I gave myself a quick heaux-bath in the sink and walked back to the bed naked. I braced myself for the shock of the cold floors, but they felt like they were heated.

Heated floors? How rich is this guy to have heated wooden floors?

As I moved closer to him, I started having second thoughts. He seemed like a really sexually open guy, but what if I went to sit on his face, and he body slammed me or something? I hesitated, lost in my own fears. But fear has rarely held me back from something I wanted to do, so I tried to get him to warm up to it in his sleep.

I massaged my inner labia and put my fingers up to his nose.

No reaction.

I massaged myself again, this time, inserting my fingers. I was turning myself on enough that when I pulled my fingers out, they were warm and wet.

Rubbing my fingers on his lips, he stirred a little, so I went full speed ahead. Since he was asleep with his mouth open, I laid my pussy-tinged fingers on his tongue. He immediately started sucking them.

"*Mmmm...mmmmmm,* that tastes good." His morning voice was a little hoarse, but that accent made me even more wet.

After he sucked all the juices off my fingers, I removed my hand from his mouth and I heard him whisper, "More, please."

I knelt on the side of the bed and straddled his neck. Without opening his eyes, he brought both muscular arms around my ass and hips and scooted my body forward so my pussy was in his mouth. He stopped, and without opening his eyes, he said, "Brandon, water, please."

Brandon showed up out-of-nowhere with a room temperature bottle of Evian. I was straddling this dude's face completely naked, and his chauffeur (who was *clearly* more than just a chauffeur) was pouring Evian into a decanter like it was brandy. Then, he poured the water from the decanter into a glass, producing a straw. Thierry turned his head to drink, while I was still straddling his face.

I covered my breasts with my hands, but Brandon had his eyes focused on the floor. Thierry was finished gulping his water (the ecstasy must have given him cottonmouth too), and Brandon moved away as if to put the glass on the nightstand.

"No, Brandon, I need one more sip of water, so I can use it on Ms. [*redacted*]."

"Yes, Mr. Jorrington," he said, obligingly.

I watched Brandon leave and couldn't help but to think that this man was fine too. The daylight really highlighted how attractive his skinny-ass was. It was like he read my mind as he closed the door. We locked eyes, and I could've sworn that he licked his lips before he left the room.

Brandon hadn't even closed the door completely before Thierry moved me back on top of his face. Shooting the water from his mouth into my pussy made me yelp in surprise. I was so turned on I couldn't tell whether it was my juices running down his face or the water he had in his mouth.

Riding faces was honestly one of my favorite things to do in life. You could tell so much about a person by how willing they are to let you potentially block their airwaves and sit on their chest. I thought I was doing some new shit, but Thierry was all about that life.

I think I may have met my match with this one.

Reaching back to grab his dick, I nearly stopped riding because I was so surprised. I must've really been high last night because I didn't remember him being this small. I couldn't see it because I was facing forward. I could only feel his full erection with my hand, and yet, I could hold the entire thing inside my tiny grip.

I was confused.

Was ecstasy that powerful to make me trip like *that*?! It didn't matter. He was using his arms to rock me back and forth on his tongue, and I could feel the pressure mounting inside me.

"Babyyyyy, don't…stop…doing…that…please. Oh, my god," I moaned.

He was moaning too, still rocking me back and forth on his tongue.

Seeing his eyes closed with pleasure made me cum so hard I clenched down and began shaking.

I tried to get off of him, but he wouldn't let me up.

He removed his tongue just long enough to say, "Let's try to get another one out of you before breakfast, yes?"

He repositioned me so I was now standing up in front of him.

"[*Redacted*], you have the most beautiful body I've ever seen. And I've seen a lot of bodies, love. It's strong, soft, and curvy." He bit and sucked my left hip before sucking his way over to the core of me. He took a long flick, inserting his tongue gently inside me and moving it until he made a circle on my clit as I shuddered.

"I don't know how long I can stand up like this." I felt my knees getting weak.

He bit me again, and, this time, sucked over to my right hip, and I was shivering from pleasure. The time he took with my body was driving me crazy.

I moved closer to his face and started grinding in a circle on his tongue. I could feel pressure rising again, more quickly than last time.

"Thierry, I'm about to, I'm about to…" He grabbed my ass with both hands and pulled me closer to him while I came for him again.

DAMN! He must've taken some pussy eating classes or something. No one had ever made me cum that fast before. Maybe the ecstasy was still coursing through my body. Either way, I was floating.

Placing my foot on the headboard, he laced one arm between my legs and one hand on my waist. He was in full control of my positioning, and there was no way I could fall now. He was sucking all the juices that came out of me and then licking slowly—so slowly that it was almost painful. The fire inside me wanted him to speed it up, but he was in complete control of my body and my orgasm. That power made the pressure build again.

There's no way I can cum again, I thought, but I did.

"You taste like musky water, and I cannot get enough. I need that ass though. Lie back down, and this time, face the door."

It wasn't like me to be compliant to any man, but I did as I was told *immediately*.

Thierry scooted down so he was on his back with a pillow propped under his head and backed me up until my ass was in his face. He inhaled deeply and took a long lick of my clit, labia, and perineum.

At this point, I was face-to-face with his dick, and it was clear that it *wasn't* the dick from last night. It was soft, but I figured, *Hell, I might as well suck it.* I mean, it was right there in my face.

I adjusted myself so I could bend down to get my balance. Getting closer, I looked at his belly, and it was wet from his own cum.

"Thierry, did you cum already?"

He was too busy munching on my asshole that all he could do was mumble.

"*Mmmhm.* I'ma cum again eating this ass." And as if on cue, he became erect again.

Oh, this dude is really on some wild-shit. He came from just eating me out. That is so hot.

I started licking his shaft and balls. 69 was not my favorite because I couldn't concentrate on giving and receiving oral pleasure at the same time, but I still did my thing.

Thierry suddenly stopped, and I felt his belly tighten.

"Oh, god, that's good." He was moaning in a different way before he went back to stimulating my anus again.

My head game was nice, even when I wasn't in a power position, and he could tell immediately, because I didn't feel his tongue moving as aggressively.

His penis was so much smaller than I remembered. I could fit the entire thing in my mouth along with a ball or two, and it drove him crazy.

"I'm about to cum, baby. I'm about to *cuuuuuum!*"

Hearing him yell like that in his accent was *wild.*

He was going *ham* on my ass, and he slowly inserted a finger. I loved a finger in the ass on occasion, and by now, he knew how my breathing changed when I was about to orgasm, but this one felt different.

"I think I'ma squirt—I'm sorry. I'm sorry. I'm…*oh, my god.*" I squirted right in his face, and he lapped that shit up like it was nectar from the gods.

Looking up, I think Brandon was watching through a small crack in the door, stroking his dick through his pants. We made eye contact again, and instead of looking away in embarrassment like I thought he would do, he unzipped his pants, pulled it out, and kept stroking. The weight of it was so heavy it just plopped out. My eyes got big as saucers because I wasn't sure if I was really seeing what I thought I was—it all happened so fast. Brandon laughed and walked away from the door.

I was so stunned from all the orgasms that I just assumed Brandon was a figment of my post-ecstasy-induced imagination and rolled off of Thierry's face before turning around to face him.

"Can you hand me a towel for my hands, love? I'd hate to rub my eye with this finger and get pink eye," he laughed. He had a very soothing energy about him.

Bringing him a towel, I said, "Damn, Thierry, you a freak forreal! That was crazy."

"Your pussy tastes so good. If I didn't have a meeting this morning, I wouldn't even brush my teeth. Girl, you are something else…I'm in town all next week. Are you going to be okay hooking up again before I head back home?"

"What? Yes, of course! This was the most fun I've had in a while. With working two jobs and trying to get into the industry, I didn't even realize how tight I was until I got to cut loose with you. What else did you have in mind?"

"Well," he started, "we have to go to Dinosaur's BBQ and then walk along the water. Wait, do you eat meat…well, I mean, besides mine," he laughed.

"Yes, I do, and I love that place. Let's play the rest by ear. I think you're going to end up spoiling me, and I won't want you to leave." I nuzzled against his neck, still puzzled about his dick situation and how he filled me up last night and how small it looked today.

"Don't start! I won't let you leave my house," he said, sexily.

I climbed on top of him and started grinding on the sheet between us.

"Maybe, I don't want to leave."

I felt his body reacting to mine. I needed to feel him inside me because I had to solve this mystery.

He started kissing me deeply, and I could taste myself. He caressed my breasts and flicked them with his tongue. Moving them together, he had both my nipples in his mouth at once. I was losing it; my nipple ring was giving me crazy sensations.

Thrashing on the bed, I moaned, "I want to feel you."

"I wanna hear you beg for it." He slipped a finger inside me while my breasts were still in his mouth.

"Please, Thierry, plea-I'm-I'm about to—"

"It's 'Mr. Jorrington' now!" Pulling his finger away abruptly, he said, "You don't get to cum yet. Hold on."

He opened the top drawer beside his bed, and I was listening for the sound of a condom wrapper, but instead, I heard a zipper. He had what appeared to be a leather, navy, toiletry bag, and he pulled out this latex contraption. He motioned for me to get off him, and he stood up with his full, yet small erection, and put the latex contraption on. There was a little loop thing for his balls, and, well, I'd be damned…this dude had a penis extender!

"Oh, wow," I said under my breath. "That is amazing! Is that…?"

"…what I had on last night? Yes," he laughed. "I've known I have a little dick for some time now. In fact, I have more than your average amount of estrogen in my system, so this might as well just be a big clit for how sensitive it is. Does that weird you out?" He had already opened a condom and somehow even the act of putting it on, watching him stroke this big black dick, was making me throb again.

"Honestly, it is a little weird, Thierry, but you already had it inside of me, so let's go!"

Smiling that beautiful smile, he grabbed my chin and gave me a kiss.

"Trust me, you'll enjoy it as much as you did last night on the dance floor."

He climbed on top of me and gave me wave after wave of orgasm, as promised.

When we were done, I asked him, "Did you take a class on how to use a penis extender? Because you are legit with that thing!"

He laughed so hard he started choking.

"No one has ever asked me that before…but, yes. I asked some of my lesbian friends who wear strap-ons to help me with my stroke. The best part is that I came almost every time you did, and there was no reason for us to stop after we caught our breath. I don't have to wait for my body to reset because I stay hard as long as you want me to."

"Damn" was all I could say, because it was a lot to take in—literally and figuratively.

I started getting dressed.

"I better get going. I have a list of things to do today."

"May I ask, like what?" He walked into the restroom to brush his teeth.

"I need to clean my house, do laundry, get groceries for the week, tell my girlfriend about the amazing guy I hung out with last night, decide if I'm going to work, etc."

"Bran…"

Brandon was there before Thierry could finish saying his name.

"Yes, sir?"

"Please, call a car for [*redacted*]. Ask Tiffany to send our cleaning and laundry service to her home and to take good care of her needs."

Brandon smiled.

"Yes, sir, Mr. Jorrington, right away."

"Thierry," I started, "I can't let you do that."

I heard Brandon making the call as he walked out the door.

"It's already done, sweetie. Let me take care of you this week, okay?" He gave me a kiss on the cheek. "Brandon has every kind of fruit you could want in the kitchen. Please, help yourself. I'm about to take a call. And text me when you make it home," he said before answering his phone. "Bonjour, Mama Brunei…"

Whoever he was talking to sounded upset, so I let myself out and walked into the kitchen, where Brandon was just hanging up the phone.

"What would you like to eat?"

"Brandon, I honestly don't need anything…but do you have a banana?" I immediately turned red from embarrassment. I hope he didn't think I was trying to come on to him.

Wait, am I trying to come on to him?

"Yes, ma'am. How about if I make you a nice smoothie?"

"That sounds great. Thank you. And thank you for scheduling those things for me; that's so kind of you."

He quickly handed me the smoothie in a glass cup with a straw and lid.

"Your car is here. Mr. Jorrington wants me to make sure you have whatever you need while he is in town. Should he be unavailable at the moment you reach out to him, you may receive a text from me if I can be of service to you."

In my post-orgasmic haze, I thought he was flirting with me a little, but I couldn't even trust my own eyes at this point. Considering the fact that I thought I saw him stroking himself while watching me have sex with his boss—my eyes were definitely playing tricks on me.

"Thank you, Brandon."

He grabbed my hand lightly and brought it up to his lips.

"You are such a beautiful woman."

"Isn't she?" Thierry appeared out of nowhere, phone still attached to his ear.

"Yes, sir," Brandon said, looking into my eyes deeply. "You have chosen very well this trip, Mr. Jorrington. Very well."

Eight

Riding home, I was feeling exhilarated from all the orgasms I had just experienced *and* exhausted from the lack of sleep. I didn't know when I put my phone on *airplane mode,* but I was glad I did, or the battery would've definitely been dead by now.

As soon as I took it off *airplane mode,* a barrage of texts started coming through.

Yesterday 8:30 PM

Shaun: Bihhhhhhh, call me back ASAP! Guess who tryna get back in these panties? Guess. GUESS! Girl, Raheem! FOH! He was lookin' good AF at the gas station though —almost unblocked his ass, but I'm staying strong, girl.

Yesterday 8:45 PM

Mama: Hi, baby, how did your work event go tonight?

Mama: I thought you'd be home by now. I know you had a long day. Was it as fun as you thought?

Mama: Miss you.

Mama: You heading to church on Sunday?

Mama: Love you.

Mama: Here's a link to a message you might like about backsliders getting right with God. Call me when you get a chance, babygirl.

Yesterday 9:10 PM

G. Money: What's good? Sorry 'bout da other night.

G. Money: DAMN, how many times a nigga gotta apologize?

G. Money: I need some of that good-good. I been missing you like crazy.

G. Money: Man, hit me back when you headed home from work.

Yesterday 9:32 PM

Shaun: Bih, where you at?! I unblocked Raheem. I think I might love him again.

Yesterday 9:45 PM

Darrell: Are you coming to work tonight?

Yesterday 10:15 PM

Shaun: Girrrrrrl...I'ma marry Raheem. He said he's changed, and I know he's my soulmate. Should I believe him?

Shaun: When he came over, he still smelled like all the weed, but he said it was because his baby mama still smokes, and he had just come from seeing his kids. You don't think he still lives with her, do you?

Yesterday 10:30 PM

Darrell: It doesn't look like it...I'm about to leave. If you're out, do you wanna grab a bite?

Yesterday 11:32 PM

Shaun: Should I fuck Raheem?

Shaun: BIH, WHERE ARE YOU? I NEED YOU! He knows all my spots, and he started feeling on me. I ran to the bathroom to call you again. WHY IS IT GOING TO VOICEMAIL?

Shaun: I know you don't like him, but if you don't call me soon, I'm about to get the dick of a lifetime. CALL ME BACK!

Today 12:07 AM

Darrell: Come on, you can't still be upset. Lol.

Today 1:45 AM

Shaun: Bitch, that dick is still too bomb. Raheem left right after though...do you think he still lives with his baby mama? He said he had to get ready for work, but now, I don't know. It's late. I'm going to sleep. Call me tomorrow.

Today 2:04 AM

Darrell: I'm taking you to brunch. I'll be there to pick you up at 11 a.m.

Oh, shit! It was 10:30 a.m. now.

I ran into the house, threw my phone on the charger, and jumped into the shower, trying to think about what I could wear that was comfortable, and not overly sexy. It was hard not to think about sex after the morning I'd had with Thierry. I got a chill underneath the hot shower, having a flashback about his mouth on my body.

Once I finished washing up and doing the "smell test" to make sure I didn't smell like latex, I was ready to go.

After drying off, I applied lotion to my damp skin. I threw on a burnt-red cotton bodycon dress with a long sweater, combat boots, and a crossbody purse. I debated on heels since Darrell was driving, but he was such a jerk, I wasn't sure if I would have to leave abruptly and walk to the nearest bus stop, so I decided against it.

I debated on texting him back at all. So many hours had passed since he sent that not-quite-an-invitation to brunch that he might've changed his mind...or maybe, he thought because I was texting right before he was due to show up that I was being a smartass.

I decided to text him just to be sure that he was actually coming before I applied any makeup.

Today 10:45 AM

Me: Okay. See you soon.

I saw the bubbles moving for a reply before I could even put my phone down.

Darrell: I'll call you when I'm out front...are you wearing heels?

Me: No.

Darrell: Good. I rarely get to see how short you really are. Lol.

"Oh, he's got jokes!" I laughed to myself. The shit was funny, considering I was wearing six-inch heels nearly every time he saw me.

I was applying the last of my makeup—just bronzer, mascara, and a light gloss—when my phone rang. It was Darrell.

"Hello?"

"Hey..." He sounded kind of uncertain. "I'm downstairs, right out front."

"Okay, I'm coming down now."

By the time I got downstairs, Darrell was out of his car, leaning on the passenger-side door. And he was looking *good* too. *Damn!* All he had on was some workout clothes and really nice sneakers. I was checking out that dick-print in his joggers, and the signal was still pretty muddled. Either way, I was no longer mad at him for #Broadwaygate. It was just good to see him.

He enveloped me into a hug, and I realized why he didn't want me to wear heels. Without them, he was head-and-shoulders taller than I was.

I rested my head on his chest, and he mumbled, "I've missed you. Let's go eat."

He didn't give me a chance to respond as he released me and went to open the car door for me. Rather than revealing what my heart felt, I just got inside.

We went to one of my favorite spots for brunch, but there was always a wait. Corner Social had great food and a bottomless brunch, so it was always a win-win.

We walked inside, and Darrell knew the guy at the door. We literally walked past everyone waiting and went right to a table.

"How did you do that?"

"I know a guy," he said with a fake Italian accent. "No, seriously…I made a reservation for us last night hoping you would respond. I'm glad you did," he smiled, and I blushed.

I didn't understand how he had this effect on me. I mean, I just spent the night with a handsome millionaire, but I raced to get ready for brunch with the assistant manager of a strip club?

What is my problem?!

"I don't think I've ever seen you during the day," Darrell said, interrupting my thoughts. "It's crazy because you have the lashes and glitter—essentially, stage makeup—on in the club, but you're honestly more beautiful here with barely any on."

He was looking at me so intently that I was beginning to feel emotional.

Swallowing the lump in my throat, I said, "Thank you, Darrell. I appreciate that."

"Well, enough with the compliments…how are you? How have you been? I've really missed you at work lately. Have you been avoiding the club because of me? I just—"

"Well, damn…can I order a mimosa first?" I interrupted.

He threw his head back and laughed.

"Yes, of course," he said, as our waitress approached our table on cue.

"May I take your order…? Darrell?! Damn, it is you! How are you? I swear, you always have a pretty girl with you whenever I see you."

He laughed, stood up, and hugged her while they exchanged small-talk for a bit before he introduced me. She offered us the bottomless mimosas with no extra charge and said she'd be back to take our food order.

"Damn, you do 'know a guy,' huh?"

"Man, that's my sister's friend from back in the day. She'll definitely take care of us," and like clockwork, she was back before we knew it.

"Here y'all go. If you can't get my attention to refill the carafe, let him know, and he'll refill it for you," she said, pointing at a busboy who was busy bussing tables. "Be right back!"

"Okay, here's your doggone mimosa. Now, let's talk."

I took a sip of the fresh tropical juice topped with champagne and started opening up as best I could.

"Simply put, Darrell…you embarrassed the fuck out of me. And then you low-key assaulted me, putting me in a damn choke hold. Even if I *did* like it, you didn't know that. I felt like you were trying to play me. And regarding my attendance at work," I drained the rest of the mimosa before continuing, "honestly, I've been working long hours at my internship and just trying to make my money stretch without having to drag my ass into work every night. I'll be back soon though. I don't want to dip into my savings too much."

I had a flashback of Thierry putting the money I would have made that night in my hand, and I wondered if he'd do that every time we linked up. My mind immediately went to the first orgasm he gave me on the dance floor, and I began to shiver.

"Hello…Nikki? Where did you go?"

I quickly snapped back to reality.

"I'm here. I'm here. Sorry, I just have a lot going on these days."

"Well," he put his head down, "I know I've said it before, but I truly do apologize. I had no idea your body would react like that or that I would embarrass you. That was not my intent. I really am sorry. Did you get my Cash App?"

"Yes, I got it. I never said, 'thank you,' did I…? Thank you, Darrell." I grabbed his hand sincerely.

"You didn't have to. I hope you accepted it with the spirit in which it was given." He placed his hand on top of mine and looked in my eyes. "Can we get back to where we were?"

"Where exactly were we?" I smirked.

Darrell looked relieved—I didn't realize how tense and hunched over he was until he sat up again. I think he liked me forreal.

He leaned in.

"…so, you squirt, huh?"

As I began to choke on my mimosa, the waitress returned.

"What did y'all decide on?"

Darrell turned to me.

"Do you mind if I order for you?"

I indicated that wasn't a problem. I liked pretty much everything on the menu, and I was anxious to see what he would order.

"Salmon eggs benedict for the lady, hollandaise on the side, please. And for me, the multigrain pancakes with a side of fresh fruit. Oh, and an extra side of bacon for the table, please."

"No problem. I'll have that out right away."

"Well, damn, Darrell. I'm impressed!"

"I did good? I'm glad…now, back to you squirting."

I blushed, continuing to laugh throughout brunch—the mimosas helped smooth out the rough patches, and I allowed myself to let bygones be bygones.

"So, are you planning to come back to work soon?"

"Yes. I'll be there tonight…as a matter of fact, I have to get home to finish my errands before the weekend ends."

Darrell paid for the meal with a generous tip and waved goodbye to his friend before we walked out. He had his hand on my waist, and despite the sensory overload from that morning with Thierry, his touch still gave me butterflies.

"I would invite you up, but," I said, as we pulled up in front of my apartment.

"I can't come up now anyway. I just wanted to take you to brunch and properly apologize to you for what happened. Now that we're back to our norm, I can rest easier."

I reached for the car handle, and he put his hand on my shoulder.

"Come here."

He placed his hand on my chin and drew my face to his, kissing me lightly on the lips. Then moving his hand over to the side of my face, I tasted his tongue on mine—gently probing inside my mouth, inquiring how far he could go.

I felt my breath catch and my pussy tingle. It wasn't a lustful kiss, but it made my heart ache.

Suddenly, he released me.

"See you tonight?"

I squeaked, "Yes" and hopped out. It was great timing too because there was a small, balding man with an empty laundry bag ringing my bell at that exact moment.

"Hi! I'm [*redacted*]. Are you looking for me?"

"Yes, I'm here to get your laundry."

"Awesome! Come on up."

I quickly threw all my dirty clothes into his bag and confirmed that I would be home later that day for him to drop them back off.

"Mr. Jorrington sends his regards."

Soon after, the cleaning service arrived. It was the best gift I never knew I wanted. Once they left and I looked around my little apartment—which had never been so clean, by the way—I danced around in my underwear because my life was great! Work was going great, a bloke with an insatiable appetite for my body had just paid for my house to be cleaned, the guy I'm crushing on took me to brunch, and I was about to go make some money tonight…how much better could life really get?

Looking down at my phone, I received a text from an unknown number.

Today 5:52 PM

(917) 426-4568: You can use my throwaway Broadway tickets and kiki at brunch all you want, but you'll never fuck my husband, you stripper bitch!

OH. MY. GOD.
My stomach dropped to my knees.
Darrell is married?!

I immediately called Shaun to give her the update on this whole Darrell situation; plus, I needed to hear this story about Raheem—whom I *despised,* but for some reason, she couldn't stop fucking with him.

"That could be anybody claiming to be his wife—a crazy ex, a current girlfriend he's tryna break up with…anybody!"

"Okay, but a crazy ex with access to his phone, or his location, or the cloud or whatever? Should I engage with her? I need to know before Darrell and I go any deeper into this thing because I almost feel like I could fall in love with him. I mean, not today, but sometime in the future…what?! Stop laughing!"

She laughed so hard she started choking.

"'I could love him.' *Really?!*" she asked, mocking me. "Girl, calm down; he just ain't giving you the dick you want, and he's got your mind going all crazy."

I couldn't help but laugh too.

"Shut up! You don't know me. Plus, it's not *just* that. He's fine, and smart, and knowledgeable," I whined. "Why won't he fuck me? It's so frustrating but turns me on at the same time," I sighed.

"Listen, you squirted in a dude's face before 10 a.m. today. I call that a win! Are you gon' text ol' girl back?"

"I'm not sure. Let me try to send you the full voicemail transcript."

(917) 426-4568: "Hello?! Does your phone not receive texts? Maybe, you'll pick up the phone instead."

When she called, I sent it to voicemail, and what I heard sounded like a lunatic.

Missed Call /Visual Voicemail
Today 5:59 PM

(917) 426-4568: "Let me guess... he picks you up in our white BMW from your little shitty apartment, most likely in Harlem since he knows everyone there and likes to impress people. Does he kiss you lightly on the lips? Order your food? Has he played with your kitty underneath the table yet...?"

Today 6:06 PM

(917) 426-4568: Lol. You are not the first nasty bitch he's done this with. He gets enjoyment out of stringing you hoes along.

Missed Call /Visual Voicemail
Today 6:15 PM

(917) 426-4568: "You're probably at a point where you want to see how his sex game is... and you've invited him into your apartment a few times, but he always declines. He declines because I told him if he ever sticks his dick inside another woman, I will take his ass to the cleaners. All his millions, properties, and businesses would be mine because I have plenty of proof of infidelity. Stop fucking talking to him, you raggedy bitch!"

Shaun gasped.

"Oh, my god, [*redacted*]. Yoooo, she sounds crazy! Even if she is lying, you might wanna leave his ass alone anyway. She sounds like the type to wait in the bushes for you with some chloroform or something—hey, look I gotta go. Raheem is outside. But before I do…did that bitch say '*millions*'?! Text me what you decide to do. Bye, love you."

"Shaun, seriously? After all Raheem's done to you, you're just letting him back into your life that easy? He gave you chlamydia, girl! He had a whole baby on you in the middle of your relationship! What is it gonna take?"

She sighed.

"I don't know," she paused, and I heard knocking at her door. "I love you. I gotta go, okay? Don't be mad at me."

"I'm not mad. I just want better for you. Love you too, friend. Go ahead and answer the door," I responded with what was hopefully not too much judgement in my voice.

I was literally dancing in my underwear only forty-five-minutes ago because everything was going so well. Now, I was pacing, biting my bottom lip in frustration. It seemed like my life had done a full 180 in less than an hour.

Darrell has a wife?

If not a wife, someone close enough to him to get access to his phone. Damn, it was like we always took one-step forward and two-steps back—I mean, I wasn't trying to be his girl *today* or anything, but damn…could we at least go out consistently without encountering some kind of issue?

Biting the bullet, I reached for my phone.

Today 6:39 PM

Me: What's your name?

(917) 426-4568: What does that have to do with you, bitch?

Me: I'm not gon' be too many more bitches. Do you want me to stop seeing your "husband" or not?

(917) 426-4568: I'm Dani—Danielle—and you can drop the quotes. Darrell is my husband.

Me: Does Darrell know that you've contacted me?

(917) 426-4568: Not yet.

Me: Good. Let's keep it that way for now. I'll see him soon, and we'll discuss it then.

(917) 426-4568: Oh, you're crazy too, I see. Lololol. Cool, I'll keep it to myself for now.

Me: Cool. Send me a photo of y'all together.

(917) 426-4568: You got a lot of nerve to be making demands, and you're the one tryna fuck my husband.

Me: Are you going to send it or not? I have things to do.

She sent a picture of Darrell and an attractive woman on a beach—with her smiling and him looking off into the background.

Me: I'll be in touch.

I found it interesting that she didn't send a wedding photo since they were married and all. Well, no matter, the trap was set. We were going to get to the bottom of this one way or another.

*****

"Hey, has anyone seen Darrell?" I'd been at work for over an hour and hadn't seen him at all. "Tonight seems kinda slow, and I wanted to know if he was willing to give me a ride uptown like he sometimes does."

"Slow? Girl, I only came back to make an outfit change because I was too sweaty to keep walking around in this other thong. If it's slow, it's because you ain't out here trying!" Peaches said. The other dancers nodded. Damn, I must've been off my game.

Coming off the stage, I got my phone, and Darrell had texted me already.

Today 11:06 PM

Darrell: Hey, Nik, sorry, I can't make it to work tonight. I had a family issue come up. We'll definitely catch up though.

Me: Okay. Be safe.

I'd be lying if I said I wasn't a little relieved that I wouldn't have to confront Darrell with this bullshit tonight. I was feeling a lot of emotions—relief, anger, all sorts of things.

At that exact moment, Thierry texted me.

Thierry: Are you bartending tonight? Where? I wanna come see you!

Shit, shit, shit! Should I tell him where I really work?

I had to consider the impact this could have on my career. If shit ever hit the fan, he could use this job as ammunition against me in some way. I hated that I was thinking that way now, but it felt inevitable with this whole Danielle/Darrell situation.

Me: I don't know, Thierry. It's pretty seedy. I don't think you'd like this place. Will you be up later though? 😜

Thierry: I absolutely will. Come through. Do you remember the address?

Me: No, but I have a great sense of direction. I will definitely see you later.

Now that I knew I'd be cumming at the end of the night, I was ready to make some money.

Ten

Heading uptown smiling, I replayed the night's events in my mind and recounted how I got my mojo back after finding out about Darrell's "wife". When I was sad or distraught about something, it always weighed me down—even things I enjoyed (like making money) are more difficult to do. My six-inch heels felt heavier, my feet started hurting faster, none of the songs the DJ played were *my* songs, and conversation didn't come as easy. I was lucky one of my regulars came in. His name was Dion aka "Chris," depending on what you believed. Dion was the name I saw on his credit card when he paid his tab the first time I sat with him at the bar, but he'd been responding to "Chris" for three-months now. Who knows what to believe…? Actually, who cares? He spent at least $300 every time he came in, and it was easy money.

I didn't see Chris at first because I was in the locker room changing into a leopard-print fringe outfit, but as soon as I hit the stage, I saw him walking to get a closer seat. I knew my night was going to get better with little-to-no work needed.

I did a basic turn on the pole, smiled my crooked smile, and slid down slowly until he was eye's length with my pussy. I had changed into a neon yellow thong, so in the dark, the outline of my pussy lips was center stage, literally. I slid my hands down my breasts and flat stomach until I got to the waistband of my thong. Sliding my hand inside, I threw my head back, mocking a self-made orgasm. As I opened my eyes, I could see every man's eyes fixated on me, but Chris was the only one I was looking at. He would spend $100 on me before I even left the stage, but he wasn't one to throw $1s.

I mouthed "Chris" in fake ecstasy and motioned for him to come closer while I pretended to play with myself. He couldn't take his eyes off my body, and I'd be lying if I didn't admit that it gave me a rush.

He gently placed two $50 bills into my G-string, whispered in my ear that he wanted a dance as soon as I exited the stage, and proceeded to wait near VIP. Other girls with better bodies would try to get to him because they saw how he spent money, but he only wanted me. The regulars had their favorites, and I was his.

I wasn't the best-looking girl there or even a great dancer, but I made these dudes feel special—one song at a time.

I didn't know what Chris did for a living, but he budgeted his money like an accountant and was straight-laced and polite like the military. Every time he came in, he knew exactly how much he was going to spend that night, and when it was gone, he would leave—sometimes, abruptly. Chris was the best type of customer; he knew what he wanted, and he didn't try to haggle.

After my set, I changed into this slutty version of a candy pink ball gown with sparkles. It fell all the way to the floor, but there were sheer panels on my ass, crotch, and breasts. This was not a dress you danced and sweated in; it was made for the wearer to be looked at, and then disrobed. Anyway, I spritzed myself with some body spray, wiped my crotch with a baby wipe since I was a little sweaty from the stage, and walked out of the dressing room into VIP.

Some of the other dancers didn't know how to code switch into faux elegance. They came in dancing fast and popping off at the guys, but not me. I agreed with mostly everything they said, let them have the last word. I basically turned into a woman from a 1950s TV show. Selling the fantasy was how I made money—having a fat ass and full titties didn't hurt either, but it wasn't automatic that men were going to spend money on me in the club because of that. This job had been a case study on human behavior in more ways than one.

I asked the bouncer outside VIP how many songs Chris paid for, and he said, "Four," so I'd be making $200 for fifteen-minutes of work tonight.

Chris paid for the fantasy—he was the ultimate gentleman and sat with his hands by his sides until I decided to placed them on me.

I sat down on his lap and whispered in his ear.

"Chris, I've missed you so much. How have you been?"

I sat his hands on my waist and stood up slowly while he rubbed my hips and ass.

"Girl, I've been missing you too. Ain't no reason for somebody to be so damn fine."

"Thank you, Christopher," I flirted. "Do you want it slow tonight…or do you wanna see me sweat a little?"

"Let's start slow…I just wanna look at you."

"Okay. Can you unzip me though, please…*slowly?*"

I turned around and looked over my shoulder as he unzipped my dress carefully from the nape of my neck all the way under my ass. And unlike most men, he didn't snatch the dress off of me—he peeled it down off my arms first, letting it fall to the floor before he folded it up very carefully. He wasn't counting the songs he had paid for because he knew he'd get his money's worth with me.

His mouth was damn-near watering.

"Christopher, is there something you want to say?"

"P-P-Please, put your pussy in my face, Nikki."

"No, Chris," I said, seductively. "I've told you before…we have to work up to that."

"Yes, ma'am," he said, accommodatingly.

"Did you think today would be the day I put my pussy in your face?" I asked, innocently.

"I was hoping so…yes, ma'am."

Psychology was one of the most understated, delicate, and important parts of being a stripper, and it could be tricky to manage at times. Men came into the club thinking they just wanted instant gratification, but you can never give in too easily, while at the same time providing a real service, or they won't keep chasing you. What they usually wanted was…intimacy.

I started to dance slowly, not to the beat of whatever ratchet rap song was playing, but to the rhythm I thought Chris wanted. Sensually looking into his eyes, I caressed my body in the ways I thought he would want to, if given the chance. And by the middle of the second song, I was standing between his legs, bending over with my breasts in his face.

"Do you want to touch me, Chris?"

I could hear his breath quicken.

"Yes, ma'am, I do."

Turning to the side, I asked, "Do you think I have a nice ass, Christopher?"

"Yes, ma'am," he said, dutifully.

I dropped down quickly and bounced my ass in front of him, bringing it up slowly so all he could see were glimpses of the pretty little pink thong hiding between my ass cheeks. I was rubbing my pussy for him when I realized that I was getting turned-on myself.

I stood back up.

"Chris, do you see this wet spot on my thong?"

Leaning slightly forward he answered, "Yes, ma'am, I do." He started rubbing his jeans where his dick was straining to get out.

"That was for you. You made me wet, Chris...do you wanna smell my pussy tonight?"

I swear, he was about to cum in his pants he was breathing so hard.

It was near the end of the fourth song, so I finally sat down on his lap, facing away from him, and rubbed against him until I felt him tense up, grab me tight, and shudder.

"Fuck. Oh, *fuck,* Nikki!"

I leaned back, feeling his manhood get soft and whispered in his ear.

"You can smell me on your pants when I leave. That's all you paid for tonight, baby. If you want more, come find me," I said, gathering my things and walking straight to the dressing room to change clothes again. I had my mojo back thanks to Chris.

As soon as he left, some music industry guys came in, and I was glad I had changed into some denim booty shorts and a bralette top—I looked like a video vixen, and that's exactly the fantasy they wanted.

When industry guys came in courting an artist, both the label and the musician would begin to feel out the other. And when it came to guys comparing dick sizes, money was often used as a measuring stick.

The rappers threw money when they heard their music playing, but the label guys weren't ones to be shown up—and it always ended up looking like a money blizzard in here. We nearly ran out of $1s, and we were all dancing on a carpet of cash.

That night, I walked out of the club with two-months' worth of my rent in my pocket and headed uptown with a smile—ready to cum as many times as my body could handle.

Eleven

When I arrived at Thierry's, Brandon was at the door in a suit, ushering me inside.

"Hello, [*redacted*]. Mr. Jorrington is on a call, but, please, come in," he said in hushed tones. "Do you need anything to drink or eat?"

I often went to bed with just a smidge of hunger after work because it was the only way I kept my stomach on flat-flat, but I didn't want to seem rude, so I asked for a piece of fruit. Brandon directed me into the dining area where I saw Thierry in what appeared to be a heated conversation out on the patio. Brandon reappeared with a bowl of kiwi, pineapple, and plums that looked so fresh, they had to have come to Harlem from some tropical location that morning. Before I could even finish my "thank you" to him, he disappeared into another room.

"...is that what you wear to bartend?" Thierry asked me, hanging up the phone as I walked in the door. I had on a burnt orange Adidas sweat suit.

"No," I laughed. "I change into something *way* more scandalous. I have to make tips with more than just my great conversational skills."

He opened up his jacket to show a burnt orange tank top—great minds and all that.

"We're dressing alike already, I see," he laughed, enveloping me in a hug. "It's so good to see you again. How was your day?"

"Honestly…?" I asked with one brow up.

He stopped what he was doing, sat down, and looked me in the eyes.

"Honestly, how was it?"

I peeled my kiwi and bit into it, chewing slowly. It was sweet and tart just like I liked it.

"…it started off great, but then it went to shit from there…wait, no, let me backup. It didn't go to shit right away. The cleaning service you sent was *A-MAZ-ING.* They were so thorough I could eat off my floors right now. Hell, I could eat off my toilet!" Thierry threw his head back, laughing. "But as I was celebrating my great day, I got a text from a guy I was dating…well, trying to date. I don't know what we *were* or *are*, but anyway, I got a text from a woman claiming to be his *wife.*"

"No way!" Thierry sat up quickly.

"Yes!"

I felt comfortable telling him an abbreviated version of this story because he wasn't my man, and he would only be in the States for another few days. He'd still be my boss' boss' boss, but we wouldn't have any interpersonal interaction, so why not keep it real? Well, *par*tially real, at least.

"So, what are you going to do?" he asked, motioning for a piece of my fruit.

"Well, I'm hoping another night with a handsome British millionaire can get my mental juices flowing, so I can figure out what to do."

Thierry pulled me toward him in the recliner and hummed.

"Is that the only type of juices you want flowing tonight?"

I took a piece of pineapple and fed it to him from my mouth. His moaning, as our tongues met around the sweet, juicy fruit, made me want to rip his clothes off right then and there.

I started to unzip my jacket and leaned deeper into him. His hands were on the small of my back, stabilizing me as I balanced on the arm of the recliner. I started grinding against the arm of the chair, unconsciously stimulating my clit as we kissed. His kisses were so deep, and I was rubbing so hard, I felt my body climaxing right there.

He whispered in my ear, "Cum for me right now," and I obliged with a muffled scream and a sigh. Standing me up on my feet, he said, "I could use a shower…how about you?"

It was like he had read my mind.

"Please, lead the way, sir."

He started disrobing on his way to the shower; by the time we got there, he was stark-naked. Even though he didn't turn on the overhead lights, there was enough to see every sinewy muscle in his shoulders and back, all the way down to his ass and hamstrings. His body was chiseled like a Greek statue.

After turning on the shower and turning around, I couldn't help but to steal a look at his flaccid penis. It was *tiny. Teeny tiny.* Itsy, bitsy, *teeny,* weeny.

The average woman has the most sensation in the vaginal opening, so data indicates that we really only need about four-inches of penis for pleasure.

Walking into the shower I thought we could try having sex without the extender, but he was definitely smaller than four-inches by my measurements. I just kept my eyes above the waist since his abs were lickable, pecs were amazing, his face was strong and masculine…and his eyes, still so mesmerizing that I could fall right into them—even in a darkened room, those gold flecks stood out. But you can't have everything, right?

Running an international company, millionaire status before 50, a smile that could light up a room, and overly generous was more than enough for me. It would've been nice, but he didn't need a massive dick too.

Thierry motioned for me to come closer and removed my shirt. My breasts were spilling out of my bra, and he hugged me, smushing our bodies together while he slipped his hands inside my pants, gripping my ass and pulling my pants down to the floor. He squatted down and removed each pant leg while I leaned on his shoulder. At this point, I was standing in a now steamy bathroom with a wet stain on my panties.

"Goddamn, you are so fine, girl." He removed my bra, started kissing me before taking my hand, as he stepped into the shower. I went to remove my panties, but he asked me not to. "I want to see them dripping wet."

He sat on a bench, watching me under a rainforest-style showerhead, and started soaping my arms, neck, breasts, legs, feet…all with my panties still on. I turned away from him to wash my face and immediately felt him behind me. He turned me around and showed me a bottle of organic feminine cleanser before putting some on his hands and began to slowly wash me. He pulled back every flap and layer of my pussy, using the handheld showerhead to get into every crevice. Watching the soap run off my body, he got down on his knees and pulled my panties to the side, giving me my second orgasm of the night with his hands held behind his back. I nearly fell over when I came without his hands grabbing my ass or thighs to stabilize me, but he caught me in time.

Once I caught my breath, he turned off the water, handed me a robe, and led me back to the bedroom. Slowly removing my panties and throwing them on the floor, he began to attach his penis extender. I honestly didn't know if I should look away or not, but I was so curious that I just kept staring.

"Thierry, that truly is an amazing human innovation."

He smiled.

"I'm glad it can bring a bit of pleasure to your shitty day…well, half-shitty day, anyway."

He put on a condom and got on top of me, using his fingers to do what his penis couldn't.

"You're still so wet, and not from the shower…see, look," he said, showing me the sticky substance from inside me. "Taste it."

I did willingly, and he kissed me as his fingers simultaneously teased me with just the tip. I moaned in his mouth; it felt so good to me.

He just kept putting the tip inside me and pulling it out. My breathing started to change, and I panted, "Please, don't stop doing that." I felt the pressure rising inside me, and as I began to cum, I felt the entire length of his girth. Moaning, he moved slowly in-and-out until our rhythm began to match and we orgasmed together.

Once we finished, I hopped up to go pee, and when I came back, he was still naked with that extender on, smiling at me.

"Thierry, I know you can keep going and going, but I have to tap out at this point. I am exhausted. What time do you get your day started tomorrow? Maybe we'll have time for another session then."

"Oh, I am so glad you said that," he said with relief, removing the apparatus from his body. "I also have to be up early tomorrow. I would definitely prefer to go to sleep as well."

Lying in his arms, I couldn't stop thinking about Darrell and what I was going to do. But gratefully, I felt sleep coming, and it was soon forgotten.

Twelve

"Thierry, I don't need anything…seriously." I was arguing with him about him giving me money.

"Just take it—don't you work hard? Don't you need a break sometimes? This is for you; do whatever you'd like with it."

Not one to argue too hard with someone trying to give me money, I took the thick envelope of cash and thanked him before I started to walk out.

"Hey," he said. "Regretfully, we may not get to do this over the next few days since I'll be taking a lot of late dinners for work…" He stopped and thought for a second. "Well, I don't know…you're a bit of a night owl, so, maybe…let's play it by ear, shall we?"

I hugged him.

"Even if we never get another chance to do…*this*, I've had a blast getting to know you better. I can't believe the owner of my company has given me multiple orgasms," I laughed. "I'll see you around the office…and having a secret like what we have will be so hot."

My face flushed just thinking about it.

He hugged me back, as he nuzzled my neck.

"Be well. I'll see you at work then."

"*Ta-ta…cheerio,* and all that."

"So silly, you are!"

Glancing down at my phone, I noticed that I had several missed calls from Darrell. I bet Danielle finally confronted his ass, and he was trying to "explain" what had happened.

"Man, fuck that nigga," I said in the cab, as I made my way back to my house.

"Excuse me?!" The cab driver nearly got into a wreck trying to swivel around to see whether I was on the phone or not.

"Sorry, not you. Please, watch the road, sir!"

Another call was coming in from Darrell, but I hit the *Ignore* button. Immediately after that, my phone vibrated in my hand, scaring me.

Today 9:09 AM

Darrell: Nikki, call me ASAP. It's urgent.

Once I got home and comfortable, I decided to call him back. Best believe, as soon as he picked up, I would be on 10. I was mad that Danielle had spilled the beans and at Darrell for lying, but fuck it, we were here now.

"Oh, you ready to explain some shit?" I said, aggressively.

"Huh?" he answered. "What are you talking about…? Anyway, do you have any personal belongings at the club?"

A bit confused, I answered, "No. I don't keep anything inside that locker; everything comes home with me, because I need to wash it often. Why?"

"Oh, good! Dream was raided last night, and everyone's things are all over the place. I was hoping you toted all your personal effects in that little roller bag you always bring."

"You weren't even at the club last night, so how do you know?"

"It's my business to know." I could hear his smile through the phone, and I smiled back instinctually.

I guess the owner notified all the manager-types.

"Did all the other girls have things there?"

"I don't know. I only contacted you. They'll figure it out the next time they come to work. So, what are you doing today? Should we do brunch again?"

Going to brunch would be the perfect opportunity for me to confront him in-person about Danielle, so I agreed.

We met in midtown for a pleasant brunch. Although the mimosas were bottomless, I was trying to pace myself. I didn't know how he was going to react, and I needed my wits about myself for this conversation.

At first, we kept it focused on what was going on at Dream, as Darrell shared some theories about one (or some) of the girls dealing cocaine from out of the club.

I told him about one girl who took a line or two during the night to stay up, but she wasn't the "drug dealer" type. She was entirely too lazy, even when she was all coked up. Apparently, the club had to stay closed during the investigation, which could take anywhere from a day up to a year.

"A *year,* Darrell? Seriously?!"

"I know. I hope it clears up soon," he nodded, as he munched on his leafy greens.

I sat back, thanking God that I had a tentative job offer at my internship, savings, and a few thousand dollars burning a hole in my pocket. Maybe, the club shutting down would help me close the book on Darrell, but I still had plans to fire into his ass about this Danielle shit.

Once our plates were cleared from the table, I said, "I think we have a mutual friend in common. I know you're not on social media like that, but I think you might know her."

I stood up to show him the photo of Danielle on my phone. Once he saw it, his entire face drained of its color. He was at a complete loss for words.

"Yeah, nigga, your *wife* called. You're a lying sack of shit, and I hate you for making me care about you!" I grabbed what was left of my mimosa and splashed it in his stupid-ass face before I stormed out of the restaurant. *Dramatic much?*

I thought I'd be fuming when I left his presence, but it felt good to actually be done with him before I made the mistake of letting him inside of me in any real way—my body or my heart.

*****

I reached out to Peaches about the raid, and she already knew, of course. She *always* had the tea! It turned out one of our customers wanted to send a message about being escorted out for improper touching. I remembered the night he was there; he kept trying to pull girls' thongs down on stage and stuff the front with balled-up dollars. He was dressed nicely in a suit like he had just come from a really good office job or something…but looks could be deceiving. Some of the nicest, most gentle guys had muscles-on-muscles with dirt underneath their nails. And the dirtiest, most entitled customers were some of the ones who made major decisions in the city, hell, even the country.

Nobody knew how he got a fake warrant, but, apparently, he worked for some high branch of law enforcement and was able to secure one with little-to-no evidence. When the police came, they completely trashed the place, finding nothing. So, they were forced to drop the *imaginary* case they had against some *imaginary* dancer. Fortunately, the owner (man of mystery that he was) was able to find out all that information, and had the place back up and running in just four-days.

I had thoroughly enjoyed this week off, only going to my internship. The money Thierry had given me really allowed me to breathe a little just like he had intended.

I went to Bel. When I saw him, I tried not to make googly-eyes at him and just kept my head down—no yawning, no coffee at the end of the day, just a regular-degular-schmegular girl working her internship.

This must be how rich people feel following their dreams with safety nets—amazing.

I shared an elevator with Thierry once.

"Hello, Mr. Jorrington, how are you enjoying your time in the States?"

"Oh, please, call me 'Thierry'. You're [*redacted*], our star intern, right?"

Karen glared at me for speaking to him, but since I had greeted him upon his arrival, I felt it would be rude not to—whether he had seen me naked before or not.

Anyway, he was very pleasant and rubbed against me a little longer than he likely had intended to upon exiting the elevator. Other than that, and a text message asking if I *"needed anything,"* we didn't really speak—which was fine by me.

I got to go home, read, sip wine, and enjoy not rushing from one place to another. I even got to meet some friends for happy hour a few times, which I never got to do anymore.

When I walked into the club on Thursday, Hyro told me that there were no bartenders there and asked me if I could make drinks. I had *no* idea what I was doing, but I said, "yes" anyway. Luckily, most people either described their drink or only wanted a shot. Knowing which glass to put things in was a little tricky at first, but eventually, I figured it out.

Although bartending wasn't my idea, it was a good one. Since it was so slow, I made more money in tips bartending in a skimpy outfit than I would dancing. Some of the regulars had heard that the police shut us down and might be visiting the club intermittently, so they stayed away.

Darrell came in towards the end of the night, I guess, to see how things were going. I didn't think he would notice me since I was behind the bar, but he walked straight up to me.

"Oh, good. I'm glad he took my advice and put you behind the bar. I know we can trust you with our money."

"Trustworthy, huh? That's more than I can say for your lying ass!"

As he threw his head back and laughed, I looked at him like he had two heads.

"What's so fucking funny?"

"You have no idea what's going on, Nik—and I probably shouldn't laugh, but when you find out the details, you'll be laughing too."

"Highly doubt it," I yelled over the music. "Well, I have customers to tend to."

He looked around.

"Customers? Where…? It's dead in here! Do you want to know the truth or not?"

I just walked away, pretending to wipe down the bar.

Looking back, I couldn't help but notice his gray sweatpants and the girth that was beneath them…good God, this man just *did* something to me.

When the night was over, I started to hail a cab when Darrell pulled up in front of the club.

"Get in and let me explain. I'll take you home."

I hesitated because he was a fucking liar, but I could've saved a lot of money by accepting the ride and not saying anything.

I got in the car, preparing to hear an outlandish tale—and that's exactly what I got.

He told some sob story about how Danielle was, in fact, his wife. And how she was bi-polar, so he didn't want to leave her...but she was manic sometimes and depressed at others and refused to take her meds. All the times he said he had to be home to care for his daughter was because he didn't want to leave her overnight with Danielle. Most of the time, his mom would come over to make sure she was okay, but she was rarely able to stay all night.

We pulled up to my apartment building before Darrell was done telling his story, and I noticed that he was anxiously playing with his keys.

"Do you mind if I come upstairs...? This neighborhood is so sketchy. Are you planning to move soon?"

"First of all, why do you care? And, secondly, do you think that sob story just secured you some pussy or something?" I asked, secretly thinking, *That sob story just secured you some pussy forreal!*

"I really need to finish this story. I need you to believe me...I see a spot right there."

He zoomed across the street to get a rare parking space directly across from my building.

Is this a sign that I really do need to entertain this dude's bullshit?

After Darrell parked, we walked inside the building together. At that moment, I was ecstatic that Thierry's cleaning company had done such a thorough job and that

I had put my clothes away instead of leaving them folded on the bed.

He walked into my apartment and said, "*Mmmm,* it smells nice in here…what is that? Lilac?" He seemed so much bigger in my little apartment than he did at the club for some reason. It was like everything inside the house bent away from him, opened up for his body to take residence there.

"Would you like something to drink? I wasn't expecting company, so I don't have much—just some white wine and cold water."

"Water is perfect. Thank you."

I directed him toward the couch and sat down about an arm's length away.

"…it's not that I didn't want to tell you. The club is just…it's like this façade; it's not real, and I didn't want to bring my real life into this 'fantasy' world. Even though we were getting closer, I just—I don't know…I should have just told you from the beginning," he spoke, haltingly, not smooth like he normally did, and my heart was bleeding at his transparency.

"Yeah, you should've told me and given me the opportunity to get to know you with that information. It doesn't help that Danielle described what we had in great detail, like you've done this plenty of times before with women just like me. I'm like, '*Woooow,* this nigga has the blueprint for serial cheating forreal,' which, knowing now what you're dealing with makes sense, but in the moment, it was mad offensive."

"What else did she say?"

I chuckled.

"She said, and I'm paraphrasing here, but that we could do all these things together, but you will never fuck me. That you're just a big tease and you get your rocks off from playing with women's emotions."

He sat there and marinated on my words for a second before he began to laugh uncontrollably—I mean, tears streaming down his face laughing, slapping his knee laughing. He was laughing so hard that I started laughing too.

"…what are we laughing at?!"

"We're laughing…" He took a breath. "…to keep from crying at the tragedy of all this," he said with his arm sweeping the room. "Danielle is right." Looking off towards the wall, he continued. "Even in the midst of her psychosis, she knows me better than anyone…we were college sweethearts, and I truly feel like we're soul mates in a way. I married her because I loved her, and she, me. And she's 100% right—I don't want to cheat on her in that way." He began to cry silently, covering his face with his hands. "I have to live too, but I don't want to completely betray her. That's why the things—the sexual things—I have done with you have been the way they have been, because I-I don't want to go too far with anyone besides her. I'm sorry for laying all this on you."

I inched closer to him and held his hand.

"I'm sorry you have to go through this alone."

Looking up from his lap with a sweet tear-stained face, he said, "I don't feel alone when I'm with you…thank you for listening." He kissed me on my cheek. "I-I wasn't expecting someone like you to come into my life and make me *feel* again. I wish there was something I could do to show my appreciation..."

I began to rub his beard with my hand, kissing his face where the tears continued to fall. Darrell opened his eyes and grazed my lips with his—lightly, like stardust. Tasting his salty tears on my lips, I kissed him back with a bit more pressure. He put his hand on my waist and pressed against my body with the passion of a man who had exhausted all restraint possible, and my body reacted with tingles everywhere.

He grabbed my face and kissed me deeply, his tongue licking my lips. As we continued kissing, he leaned into me more, and his hand went down from my face to my neck where his mouth followed—first, flicking my neck with his tongue and up to my earlobe where he growled, "You must've worked hard tonight! You taste like sweat…I like that shit."

The realization that he was really here with me, on top of all that he was doing to my body, made me shudder with pleasure. Can women have pre-cum? Like a pre-orgasmic experience? I didn't know for sure, but it certainly felt like it.

"Damn, baby, it's like that?"

I nodded.

"Yes, for you, it is," I moaned, as I looked him straight in the eye. "Let me feel you, Darrell."

It was like those five words flipped a switch inside him, and he became a sex animal! Usually, he was in total control of his environment, but perhaps, more importantly, he always seemed to be in control of *himself.* I could tell that he was totally letting go with me.

His hand went back to my throat as he kissed me deeply—his tongue intertwining with mine. It felt like he was searching for something deep inside me…probing, looking for answers or a pleasure-center of sorts. I allowed him inside me, to scan my recesses as deeply as his tongue could go until he found what he was looking for. As he gripped my throat with one hand and continued to kiss me, I could feel him stiffen on top of me. At this point, I was so turned-on I wasn't sure if there was a puddle beneath me.

While kissing me, he removed my pants and whispered, "I've wanted to taste you since the moment you walked into Dream...may I?"

"Of course, you can," I said, stroking the back of his head gently.

He took a pillow from off the couch for his knees, lifted my shirt, kissed my stomach softly, and then, with more pressure on one side than the other, he began to tease me. When he used his entire tongue to lick one side of my stomach, I was breathing so hard I wasn't sure if I was going to survive this entire experience or not.

Darrell was back in control, taking his sweet time, and I was loving it.

He looked up at me.

"Are you okay? You're breathing so hard." He sounded genuinely concerned, but there was a twinkle in his eye.

"Yes," I huffed. "Please, don't stop."

He flicked his tongue along the top of my panties, and I was going crazy. I didn't even know I could be aroused with attention in that area.

After making me squirm for what felt like forever, Darrell kissed my pubic bone through my panties, grabbed my right thigh, pulling my legs further apart to lick along the place where my panties met my thighs.

He started nibbling on my thighs and smelling me, moaning with pleasure after every inhalation.

As he got closer and closer to my center, I could feel an orgasm building inside me, but I really didn't want to cum that fast for him. I wanted to make him wait, like he had made me wait. But the waves were hitting the shore, and I couldn't stop the pressure from building.

"Your musk is making me so fucking hard. You must have some crazy pheromones, girl. Damn!" he said before he dove back in, still on top of my panties.

He reached for my face to kiss me and began to rub his thumb on my now throbbing clit, pulling my panties to the side so I could feel actual skin-on-skin.

I gasped in his mouth and grabbed his back; the waves were building higher, and I couldn't hold back anymore.

"Darrell, I'm cumming," I whispered, and he kissed me deeper as I came on his hand.

"Now that we have that out of the way, we can really get started," he said with a mischievous grin.

Pulling my panties to the side, he enveloped my entire pussy in his mouth and did tricks with his tongue that I had never experienced before. I quickly squirted in his mouth, and he just kept going and going and going.

Finally, he said, "Please, tell me you have some condoms."

"Yes, in my room in the nightstand," I answered, breathlessly.

"Don't move a muscle."

I laid there half on the couch, half off the couch, panties askew, shirt lifted up, and titties half out of my bra. Darrell was back in a flash with his pants folded nicely in his hand.

I sat up, and my eyes nearly jumped out of my head.

"NO…FUCKING…WAY. You've been walking around with *that* this whole time?!"

His penis was beautiful.

It was the color of brown sugar slowly melting on a stovetop, like it had the "glow" (sho nuff!), or maybe just the aura of sex was emanating from it. I didn't know.

I swear, he was walking toward me in slow motion, swinging his dark, shiny dick in my direction. As he got closer, I could see that vein pulsing, and my mouth started watering. It had the girth of a summer sausage and was a solid six-seven-inches long.

I licked my lips as he pulled off his shirt and got back down on his knees, pulling my panties to the other side, and going to town like the wet spot on the couch wasn't even there. He started nibbling and groaning with my pussy in his mouth. Pulling away from me with a smirk on his face, he ripped my thin, lace panties off my hip so they were hanging on one side.

Grabbing my ass with both hands, he lifted me up, so my knees were damn-near on my forehead. I held onto the edge of the couch cushions, curious as to what he was going to do next.

He put his nose on my perineum and inhaled deeply before giving my ass a lick. Moaning with pleasure, he moved his head around and around as he pleasured my anus, eventually letting my legs down and focusing back on my clit…until I came for him again.

"Fuck this shit," I heard him say, as he ripped open the condom wrapper and put it on. "I need you…right now."

He put my legs down, so I was lying on the couch properly before he climbed on top of me. Wrapping my body in his arms, he started kissing me deeply, and I felt him rubbing against me—the friction against my clit along with his dick against my stomach as we rocked felt *sooo* good.

I felt him pull away enough to gain entrance to my wetness, and without using his hands, the tip of his penis was inside me—stretching me just enough for it to hurt a little, and I yelped.

He stopped.

"Are you okay? I don't want to hurt you anymore…"

I kissed him.

"I'm more than fine. Please, don't stop"

Darrell rocked the tip right inside me until I felt a wave coming; he must've felt it too because at the moment, I began orgasming. He let me feel the entire length of him inside me. Gasping from the increased sensations, along with the intensity of being with a man I had lusted after for so long, made me cry. He rocked inside me and kissed my tears, the way I had kissed his.

Eventually, he pulled me on top of him and took off the rest of my clothes, so we were both completely naked. He held me so tight I could hardly get a good rhythm. He seemed to get more enjoyment from the closeness than the friction.

Finally, he let me go so I could give him a proper ride.

Feeling my heavy ass bounce on his thighs while I licked his neck and nibbled on his ear was driving him to the brink of ecstasy. I could feel his breath quicken.

"If you keep doing that, I'm not gonna last much longer," he gasped between breaths.

He was about to cum, and I wanted to see what his face looked like when it happened. I had waited this long—I *had* to see and feel *every*thing.

"Oh, my *fuuuuuuck,*" he screamed, holding me as tight as humanly possible. "Stop…don't move." He held his head back in ecstasy—that point between pleasure and pain after a man cums and doesn't want to feel you tighten the pussy around him or move too much. That part was hilarious to me, but I honored his request and stopped moving.

"This, this is why I didn't want to sleep with you—the chemistry between us is too wild…there's no coming back from this." He kissed me sweetly before grabbing the blanket that was draped behind him and wrapping us inside it with me still on top of him.

Maybe, today wasn't so bad after all…

Thirteen

"What are you looking at?" I asked, blushing, trying to keep my breath inside my mouth. I woke up, and Darrell was watching me sleep.

"I rarely get to see you in the daylight—you are so beautiful." The light was coming through my blinds, and while I doubted that I looked like Sleeping Beauty, I didn't take off my makeup from the night before, so I probably looked better than I typically would have first thing in the morning.

"Wait until I wash my face, then decide if I'm beautiful," I said, sarcastically.

"Last night was so good, girl. Damn…" He pulled me in close, and his touch transported me back to the night before instantly—two sex sessions with multiple orgasms and an intensity that was unmatched to anyone *ever*.

"I agree," I said, enthusiastically. "Now, let me go brush my teeth…hey, how does your breath *not* smell?"

"I got up and got an apple while you were snoring. It's nature's breath freshener—try it," he said feeding me a slice of apple, and it really worked.

Chewing slowly, basking in the afterglow, my mind started racing with a thousand questions.

"So, about last night…how do we move forward? I mean, you're *married*…not divorced or separated like you told me at the club. Yeah, this was great, and clearly, we have an intense connection, but you're a bit of a prick if I'm being honest."

He looked so offended and hurt, but I let my statement stand.

"[*Redacted*], I'm sorry. I just, I felt like there was no need to be honest with someone I met at a place like that."

"A place like that? Like what? The strip club? Where everyone is hustling? Where women are the *most* vulnerable, yet the most *valuable* asset to your business? Man, fuck outta here!"

"Come on, you know that's not what I meant—you also know everyone is not like you there. You're on some other shit; you have a college degree for God's sake!"

"Whatever," I said. My after-sex-glow was diminishing by the second.

Darrell sat up and turned his back to me with his head in his hands.

"Listen, I like you. You're smart, beautiful, and funny…can we just do what we've been doing?"

"Are you gonna 'just do' your marriage?"

Just then his phone rang.

"Tell Danielle I said, 'hello,'" I pouted as I stomped out the room, slamming the door to the bathroom behind me.

How can he take a call from his wife in the middle of our argument?

Suddenly, a few gunshots rang out as Darrell was talking. Maybe, it was time to move. I never really paid attention to how dangerous my neighborhood really was.

My heart melted hearing pieces of Darrell's conversation through the door.

"Hi, honey! I miss you too. Are you having fun at Grandma's house…? You wanna go to the movies today? Okay, I'll be over to get you this afternoon. You being good…? Love you, babygirl."

Damn, he was talking to his daughter? How am I supposed to stay mad after a conversation that sweet?

Running out, I jumped on him, pushing him on the bed playfully. He grabbed my waist and mumbled, "I'm glad you're not mad at me anymore—you see, my daughter will always come first because she really only has one parent right now."

Kissing his neck and ears, he started moaning.

"…don't start nothin' you can't finish." He reached for my ass with both hands and started grinding my body against his.

"No, I'm in control now," I said, grabbing his hands and pinning them to the bed while I grinded against him and sucked on his neck. I let his hands go and went down towards the foot of the bed, kissing his chest. His nipples were super sensitive, so I spent a fair amount of time on them, listening to him moan and feeling him squirm beneath me. Moving down toward his pelvis, I licked everywhere the sun touched until his dick popped up, nearly hitting me in the face.

I had to get a good look at it, and it was even more beautiful in the daytime.

I caressed it and kissed it like we were meeting for the first time. I got off the bed and onto my knees for better positioning. Darrell must have read my mind, because he handed me a pillow, which brought me up an inch. I needed to get to *everything*.

Holding his manhood with my right-hand, I licked up the shaft where his vein was throbbing and gently played with his balls with my left. I was teasing him, never allowing his dick all the way into my mouth.

I moved it out of the way and started sucking on his balls very gently—first the left one, then the right. I swirled my tongue in a circle on each until I began to make a figure eight. I felt his abs tense up and his breathing become shallow.

I did one last figure eight on his balls before I licked up his shaft and opened my mouth just wide enough to barely fit him inside of me. Hearing him whimper beneath me made me nearly squirt—*almost*. I had to remain in control, so I didn't allow the wave to wash over me…not yet.

I held my mouth tight like a virgin's pussy, making him fight his way inside and into the back of my throat, initiating my gag reflex and producing more spit. Coming up the shaft, I relaxed my mouth and went up and down slowly, moving my hand in a circular motion—up-and-down, up-and-down. I couldn't tell if my mouth was watering from my gag reflex or because his dick was so fucking tasty in my mouth. Either way, I allowed the spit from my mouth to fall on his dick. I watched it travel down the shaft and onto the balls slowly. I hoped he could feel that sensation alone, and I thought he did because he shivered as it traveled down.

Gobbling up the extra spit from his balls and going up the shaft and into my mouth, I felt him tense up.

"Baby, I can't hold it. I'm cumming for you."

I hummed on his dick, adding a hand to go up and down with my mouth, as I tasted salty, sweet, semen hit my jaw. I let it fall out of my mouth and back onto him while he lay there seemingly lifeless.

"Darrell?" I shook him. "Darrell…?" I was starting to panic. Did he have some kind of heart condition; had I sucked out his soul?

"*Gahhh*damn, girl."

He opened his eyes and grabbed my face, kissing me deeply.

"You can't be doin' that shit first thing in the morning; you gon' have to kick me out."

I laughed.

"I thought you were dead!"

"Shit, damn-near. You 'bout killed me!"

We laughed together before he got up to get a warm towel.

"I would let you return the favor this morning, but I have to get ready for work."

"I understand completely," he said. "Listen. I like you—let me spoil you, okay? I just, I have a situation that's not optimal right now, and, honestly, I don't see it changing anytime soon—but you…you are *not* a secret. I've told everyone about you; they know my marriage is only to keep our family unit together and not for love, and they want me to be happy…I hope you feel the same way."

Looking down, I knew I couldn't give him the answer he wanted.

"Darrell, I—"

He interrupted.

"Just think about it okay…?"

"Okay," I said, as I hugged him. "Now, get out!"

After he left, I instantly called Shaun.

"*Bihhhhhh,* wake up! You are not going to believe the night I just had…"

Fourteen

By the time I got to work, I had a text message.

Today 9:04 AM

Darrell: Hey, would you consider being a bartender full-time?

Me: I don't know...I may not even need that job much longer, depending on how my internship works out.

Darrell: Lol. People who take home hundreds of dollars tax-free don't go into Corporate America without keeping a toe in the nightlife. BELIEVE ME. Haha...but I understand either way. Think about it though. Seriously—you would be great at it!

My desk phone was ringing, and the caller ID matched the office Thierry was using this week.

"Bel internship workroom, this is [*redacted*]. How may I help you?"

Thierry laughed.

"…so formal! Hey, [*redacted*], please, call all the interns into Conference Room 1. I need to speak with everyone."

"Right away, sir…"

I could still hear him breathing on the other line.

"…is there anything else I can do for you, Mr. Jorrington?" I asked with a veiled innocence, hoping he could hear the lust in my voice.

"Yes, you can sit that supple ass on my face and cum in my mouth…is that something you're willing to do?"

I was so surprised that I started choking and laughing from embarrassment.

By this time, the other interns had started walking into the workroom, so acting normal was a *must*.

"No, sir, I am unable to do that at this time, but, perhaps, once we have all the tools available, we could possibly revisit…I'll gather everyone into the conference room shortly." I hung up before he could say anything else crazy that would cause me to react in front of my fellow interns.

Once I gathered everyone, we walked into the conference room, and his fine-ass was already there with Emily, Karen, and a few other higher-ups in the company. They all stood quietly, looking at different things, as the six of us interns stood there.

"Mr. Jorrington, you asked me to assemble all the interns." I was slightly nervous that something bad had happened. The last time they asked us to come together like this, it was after that beautiful pageant winner jumped off her patio. They had grief counselors on standby in case people wanted to talk.

"Yes, yes," he said, turning around, smiling. "You all have been amazing this past week. I know I've asked for a lot of challenging things, and with all the late nights…today is my last day at the U.S. office, and I just wanted you to know that you're all greatly appreciated."

He grabbed a stack of envelopes from his desk with our names and handed them to us one by one.

"This is just a symbol of my gratitude to all of you for this week and what you do for this company. Lunch will be catered today, specifically for you."

The rest of the employees on the floor had gathered behind us with smiles and applause, yelling, "Thank you" too and giving lots of hugs.

"There's one more thing I'd like to say…or maybe, Emily, would you like to?"

Emily stepped forward.

"As you all know, [*redacted*] is always the first to arrive and the last to leave. She's given clear insight on many projects and has always gone the extra mile with our company. Please, give a special 'thank you' to [*redacted*]—our *star* intern this year!"

I was so caught off-guard; tears sprang to my eyes. All the other interns (even the jealous ones) started congratulating and hugging me.

"Wow, thank you, everyone," my voice wavered. "It's not easy working every day and night, but I wouldn't do it for any other company."

Even Karen found it in her cold heart to turn her mouth into the semblance of a smile and shake my hand.

Thierry found me and gave me a hug.

"Congratulations—you deserve it! I hear a job offer is coming soon too," he said in my ear. "Make sure you open your envelope when you're alone."

The other interns started opening their envelopes to thick stacks of cash and started squealing and hugging each other, discussing what they were planning to buy with their windfall.

When I finally got to my desk to open mine, there was a stack of money inside and a key.

Meet me at my place tonight, please. I've missed you tremendously.

I had planned to work tonight, but fuck it…this man was only in the country for one more night…maybe, I could do both.

I quickly texted Thierry.

Today 2:45 PM

Me: Will you be up when I get off work?

He immediately texted back.

Thierry: I will...or maybe, I'll just come to your job instead.

I didn't want his last image of me to be at the strip club, but I couldn't pinpoint exactly why. As confident as I was in my decision to dance, maybe, I still felt a little anxiety about telling anyone who knew me from the "real" world.

Would Thierry still see me as someone hustling, or would the environment change that perception?

Sexuality as it pertained to Thierry was okay, but seeing that same strong sense of sensuality displayed with a complete stranger…I didn't know if that would change the dynamics of our "relationship". Intense sexuality could intimidate men; they were turned-on by it until they realize they didn't "bring out the freak," but that I *chose* to exhibit this sensuality—it had nothing to do with their power.

I didn't feel like thinking about it so deeply; plus, there was so much to be happy about.

Today 2:50 PM

Me: No, that's okay. I'll just come to you afterwards.

*****

When I showed up to work that night, Darrell was on me right away.

"Zamn, Zaddy, stop sweatin' me," I laughed.

He smiled.

"Have you given any more thought to bartending? I could really use you behind the bar tonight."

"Shit, Darrell…to be honest, I haven't had time to really think about it—I'm sorry. I'll have an answer for you by tomorrow. Is that okay?"

He furrowed his brow, but smiled.

"Yes, Nikki, that's fine. See you on the floor out there."

For a Friday night, it was pretty slow. After making my rounds with all the customers, I went into the dressing room until it was my turn to hit the stage. As I was changing clothes, some of the girls came back giggling. I could only hear pieces of their conversation, but it seemed to be about a customer.

"Hey, y'all. Somebody come in spending tonight?"

"*Biiitch,* yes! This fine-ass nigga just walked in asking for $1,000 in $1s."

"I saw him walk into VIP with Cocoa just now."

"Damn, I hope he's out of there by the time I hit the stage. I barely made tip out tonight."

Cocoa was a baddie, and kept customers spending money song after song. I doubted this stranger would be out on the floor by the time I hit the stage, but I changed into something a little flashier than I had planned—just in case.

After changing into a hot pink hooded one-piece that slid between the crack of my ass perfectly, I heard my name and hurried to the stage. I started my routine and saw the door to VIP open out of my peripheral vision.

"Good, maybe, this guy will want to spend money on the stage as well as private dances."

I looked up, and Thierry was standing at the edge of the stage just smiling.

"Well, hello, [*redacted*]."

My heart skipped a beat, but my feet didn't miss a step.

"Hello, Thierry. Call me 'Nikki' here, please," I whispered into his ear. "What brings you out tonight?"

"I could lie and say that I googled 'premiere strip clubs NYC,' but the truth is I've known where you worked since night one. You said it while you were high on E our first night together."

I threw my head back, laughing.

"No way! Are you serious?" I doubled over laughing so hard I could hardly dance because I couldn't believe that I was actively trying to keep a secret from him that he already knew.

By this point, I was dancing in front of him while he was dropping cash below me.

"…Nikki, come back to London with me. I have trips planned to Abu Dhabi, Singapore, Paris, and other places in the next few weeks. Being with you would make the work a little less…*strenuous.* Give it some thought. I'm going to get a few more lap dances; you have beautiful colleagues."

"Make sure you make time for me to give you one too, sir," I chuckled.

Looking down, there was at least $200 beneath me—just for a two-minute conversation on stage. Sometimes, this job could be very lucrative.

I'd just finished gathering all the ones from the stage when I heard someone yelling. New Yorkers always seemed to be aggressively yelling at one another, but this was different.

As the DJ transitioned into a new song, I heard, "WHERE THE FUCK IS NIKKI?! IS THAT THAT BITCH RIGHT THERE?"

I turned my head toward the ruckus to see a woman who had to be "Danielle". She was walking menacingly toward Peaches, who had begun removing her earrings and taking her heels off, ready to throw hands with whoever had an issue with her.

Dani was a beautiful woman dressed in pajamas and a fur coat that draped to the floor. Her hair was disheveled, and she wore flip flops despite the dropping temperatures outside. Beautiful looks aside, you could tell something wasn't all the way right with her mental state.

Darrell came running out from the back.

"Dani, what are you doing here?" He grabbed her arm and tried to escort her towards the door. "You can't just come to my place of business acting like this! Did you take your medication today?"

"Fuck you, Darrell. Fuck you…and your stupid club…and your stupid whore…and your stupid money! I don't care that you own this place. You're still an 'ain't shit' nigga!"

I exchanged a look with Peaches that said, *He owns Dream?!*

Dani continued.

"You think because you're a millionaire that you can control me with your bullshit schemes, but you can't! I didn't take my medication today, and I DON'T GIVE A FUCK ABOUT IT!"

She clearly wasn't having a good day.

"Now, where…is…Nikki?"

Walking up to her, I spoke up.

"I'm Nikki. What's good?"

"'What's good?' You sneaky fucking bitch!" she screamed over the music. "I told you he was married, and your response to that was to go and fuck him anyway? I smelled you all over him when he walked through the door!" She lunged at me, but I had been walking, running, and dancing in six-inch heels for a few years now, so my core was crazy strong.

I dodged her, and she quickly fell to the floor.

"Listen, Dani," I started.

"It's '*Mrs.* Hutchins' to you, *skank!*"

"Dani, listen" I said, squatting down so I could talk directly into her ear. "He's your husband to control, not mine. You're embarrassing yourself right now, so stand up and walk out of the front door like a woman with some dignity."

She lunged at me again—this time, making contact with my shoulder. But she fell over again as I dodged her.

"Nik, you gon' let her try and clown you like that?"

"Let her ass fucking have it!"

"Tag me the fuck in; I've been waiting to beat a bitch's ass!"

"Fuck her up, Nik. What you waiting for?"

My co-workers were trying to gas me up, but based on my conversation with Darrell, I knew Danielle wasn't right in the head, and I wasn't trying to put her down like that.

"Darrell, come get your wife, man—she don't want it with me."

Darrell moved carefully toward Danielle, trying to envelope her into a hug, but she struggled away.

"You love her?" she asked with tears in her eyes. "You gon' do what she says? Is this what it's come to?"

Darrell pulled her closer, and I saw her pull out something shiny—a *knife!*

"Darrell, watch out!" I screamed, but it was too late. Before he could grab her wrist, she stabbed him in the hand where the knife was now sticking out.

"*Darrellllllll!*" Danielle gasped louder than any of us, yelling, crying, and hugging him like she wasn't the one who had just stabbed him. "I'm sorry. I'm *so, so* sorry. I'm sorry, baby. I love you. I need to go back to the doctor, right, baby? Let's go. I'm sorry. Don't call the police again, okay? Please?"

By then, the DJ had turned off the music, and we heard most of their conversation as they walked out the door. All my girls surrounded me, giving me hugs and asking if I was okay. Peaches eventually yelled, "turn the muthafuckin' music back on." We still had work to do.

When I turned around, Thierry was behind me with a concerned, yet comical look on his face.

"*Sooo,* this is work as a 'bartender,' eh?"

Despite the stress I was feeling, I couldn't help but laugh.

"Yes! Take me to VIP *now,* please! I need to get out of here."

I towered over him in my heels, but he took my hand and led me into VIP, paying the bouncer for five songs.

"I can tell you need a break, love. Come on!"

When we walked into VIP, I leaned over him, becoming a stripper caricature of myself.

"What kind of dancing do you want, baby?" I asked, making sure my boobs were in his face, but all he could do was laugh.

"[*Redacted*]…or 'Nikki,' is it? Please, have a seat. Take your shoes off and swing them over to me."

I did as I was told, and he started massaging my feet.

"Thierry, OMG, that feels so good…and you don't even have any lotion!" He cracked each toe for me, smiling.

"I used to massage my mum's feet every night when I was growing up. Now, just relax and enjoy getting paid to get a massage while I talk to you…I've missed you so much this week, seriously, and I don't want this to be the last time I massage you."

My eyes were closed in ecstasy.

"*Mmmm*…well, come back to the States more often so we can hang out," I murmured.

"…do you have a passport?"

My eyes shot open, and my feet hit the floor.

Was he really serious about the proposition he made on the side of the stage? Is he trying to make this thing more official?

"Yes, I have a passport, but I can't afford to travel right now, especially if I get this job…I won't have any vacation days, and—"

"*Shhhhh.*" He stopped me, holding out his hands for my feet to continue their massage. "You're going to get the job offer Monday. I've made sure of it."

"Wait, what do you mean…?"

"No, no, no, no, not in a creepy *'I'm fucking this woman, so give her a job'* way, but in a *'she's the best intern we've ever had,'* and a *'you'd be crazy not to hire her before someone else scoops her up'* kind of way," he said, laughing over my feet.

Still, if anyone ever found out that I was sleeping with the boss, my credibility would be shot— I had to play this right.

"You're going to get the job offer on Monday; and naturally, you'll accept it. But you'll need some time to go home, visit family, and adjust to having a real job, so give your other job," he said, sweeping his arm around the room of the club, "enough notice that you're leaving. You'll need at least six-weeks before you start—you will train the other interns to pick up the slack in your absence, and you can start with fresh ideas, ready to roll, and won't require a vacation until next year, sometime."

"*Six-weeks?!* Are you insane? They are not going to let me do that!" I pulled my feet down and put them back into my heels, standing abruptly.

"You won't know until you try," he smiled, looking up at me. "Women tend to downplay their own power. They want you! And they don't want all the things you've learned about the industry to go to a competitor. If they don't meet your demands for six-weeks, they'll at least give you a month…and after you fly home to see family, I'd love to fly you to meet me somewhere in the world. Are you down for that…?"

I didn't have to think at all.

"*If*—and that's a *big* 'if'—*if* they offer me the job, and then *if* they allow me off for four-weeks, then, *duhhh!* Yes! Yes! Travelling with you? A gazillion times, 'yes!' And, honestly, I just went home to see my family for the holidays. If I get the job offer, and *if* they accept my terms, I'll text you right away so we can make plans." I sat on his lap and hugged him with tears in my eyes. "That would be a perfect next step to the bullshit going on here—a chance to reset would do me a world of good."

"I hope to do you good later tonight," he smirked, motioning towards the ceiling. "Do those cameras work?" He pulled me off him and motioned for me to sit beside him again.

"Sometimes. Usually, we can tell if someone's watching by how the camera moves. Go walk toward the door and see if the camera follows you."

He got up to walk, and it didn't move. With all the drama going on outside, I was sure no one was even paying attention to VIP.

Unzipping his pants, he grabbed my foot again, putting my big toe in his mouth; he sucked on it until he got it really wet, grabbing his dick with his other hand. He started touching himself while sucking my toes. I could see him getting hard, and it was turning me on like crazy! Even though he had the smallest dick I had ever seen, something about him was so sexy.

When he placed my feet on his dick, despite never doing anything like this before, I started jacking him off, and it was hot!

"Your feet are so fucking beautiful," he kept saying over and over, looking down at his dick and my freshly pedicured, candy pink, toenails.

As we started song five, he came all over my feet, took off his scarf, and wiped it up.

"I can't believe I just did that," I said, breathlessly. "I could get fired!"

"Yes, you just did that," he laughed. "And when you come over, I'ma do you."

We walked out of VIP laughing, arm in arm. Darrell was by my side in a flash.

"Hey, Nik, are you okay?"

"I'm cool. You're the one bleeding," I motioned toward his hand.

"It's not as bad as it looks," he said, sheepishly.

"*Nik,* I'll see you later, okay?" Thierry said, as he began to walk away.

"Hey, ask for 'Peaches'. She'll get you *all* the way right," I said, as he walked away. Less than a minute later, I saw him walk by with Peaches as they entered VIP together.

"Nik…*Nikki,* are you listening to me?" Darrell was scanning my face for a reaction, but I refused to give him one.

"Listen, Darrell, Rules #8 and #10 were broken by both of us…let's not draw any more attention to ourselves, okay? Although, I guess 'rules' don't really matter when you're the *owner,* huh?" I rolled my eyes.

He looked hurt.

"I understand…I'm headed to the hospital, so they can check out my hand. Text you later? I can explain everything—why I didn't come clean about owning the club and stuff, okay?"

I looked past him without any expression.

"Sure, whatever…ultimately, you're just a liar though. What more is there left to say…?"

In the cab headed to Thierry's house, I made a *pros/cons* list concerning his offer.

PROS	CONS
1. See the world FOR FREE.	1 Missing out on things go-ing on stateside
2. Exposure to different cul-tures	2. Leaving Darrell during a really stressful time. (Should this even be on the list?)
3. Exposure to a lifestyle I may never see again in my lifetime.	3. Thierry could be a serial killer.
4. Thierry only wants to have fun and is low stress.	
5. Possible inside information to the industry and a GOAT to bounce ideas off of	
6. Access to nearly anything I could ever want.	

Aside from Thierry being a possible, theoretical "Killer," there was really no reason for me not to go. I was 89% sure I was going, and I started getting really excited about it.

When I got to the house, Brandon escorted me inside.

"Hello, miss. Please, excuse the disarray while we get packed up to leave…I saw Thierry lying down on the couch on his phone."

"*We?*" I laughed, and then I heard other voices. There was a full staff of people packing up, labeling things, itemizing documents—anything and everything you could think of.

Brandon smiled.

"Yes, *we*."

I laughed nervously, realizing my mistake, and walked over to Thierry, straddling him on the couch. I grabbed the blanket and threw it around my shoulders like a cape. I was chilly.

"Mr. Jorrington," I said with a terrible British accent, "shouldn't you be helping to pack?"

"Oh, but I am. Brandon told me a few years ago that all I do is get in the way and mess things up. That same year, he requested that he and the staff handle *all* the labeling and packing, and everything went so smoothly. I've stayed out of the way since. They like it better this way," he laughed. "Anyway…" He grabbed my ass. "Regarding my departure, should I be expecting some company soon?"

"I thought about it the whole way here, and I have to know…why me? I'm sure you have your pick of women who would love to accompany you places and do all the nasty shit you like to do, so why *me?*"

Thierry thought briefly and smiled.

"Brandon, can you come here, please?"

He was there in a flash.

"Yes, Mr. Jorrington, sir?"

"Can you tell Ms. [*redacted*] why I want her to travel with me? Tell her what I told you, please."

"Mr. Jorrington, are you sure, sir? That conversation was, *ahem*...quite intimate."

"I'm sure," he laughed.

"...he said you had the sweetest pussy he's ever tasted, he hasn't made you cum enough times yet, and you only laugh at things that *truly* amuse you..." Brandon looked embarrassed. Hell, I was embarrassed for him.

"Don't forget the last part, Brandon," Thierry coaxed.

Brandon looked pained to say it.

"He said that his money is long, and while you won't try to separate him from it, you don't pretend to feel bad for spending it either."

"Thank you, Brandon. I won't hold you up any longer." Turning back to me, he said, "You have a hustler's spirit about you, but that's not all that you are. It can be difficult for wealthy men like me to discern women's intentions—some act like they don't care about money when they actually care very deeply. Others *only* pursue me because of my money. You are a balance of self-awareness, selfishness, and selflessness. I appreciate the person who's currently straddling me, and I just wanted to spend more time with you. That's all...you weren't expecting that, I assume?" It must have been written all over my face.

"I-I'm flattered, really and truly," I stammered. "I know that was real, and I appreciate your honesty...one last question though—what happens when you begin to tire of me or vice versa?"

He looked perplexed.

"How does a woman like you think any man will tire of you? You have no idea how charming you really are, do you?" He was looking at me with those eyes again, and I felt my heart prickle. Could I have real feelings for Thierry too? No way! This was just a novelty thing.

"...but let's say you do eventually tire of a life of travel and partying, I'd ask how soon you'd like to get back to the States. Brandon would book a flight and get you home ASAP. It's clear that you still have deep feelings for Darrell, so I promise not to fall *deeply* in love with you when you visit. We'll just have the time of our lives instead."

"Are you sure you won't fall in love?" I laughed. "Seriously though, this sounds like an amazing vacation. And as soon as I get that job offer and they accept my terms, I'll be there on the first thing smokin'!"

Thierry brought my face down to his to kiss me, before he went under my pants, grabbing my bare ass. I immediately responded to his touch on my skin as he went lower and lower until I felt one finger nearly inside me. The other rubbed against my clit, making me moan into his mouth while we kissed.

"I bought this earlier today," he said, producing a light-blue vibrating bullet-shaped sex toy. He turned it on to its lowest level, and despite his whole team hustling and bustling around us, underneath the blanket, he reached back under my pants. I gasped, feeling the vibrations immediately on my clit.

Thierry went back-and-forth awkwardly between my clit and pushing it inside me, just deep enough to activate my pleasure center. I was 100% sure the staff knew what was going on, but that just turned me on even more. In fact, I swore I saw one of his employees looking in our direction intentionally as she dipped off to the restroom. I was so caught up in my orgasm I couldn't really be sure.

I tried to stifle my cries against his chest, but my body betrayed me as the waves crashed over me. I was sure the blanket around us looked crazy because I was shaking uncontrollably.

"Damn, I wish those juices were on my face right now," he whispered in my ear as I was reaching the peak of my orgasm. There was no denying the sexual chemistry between us—I just assumed he was like that with every woman he was with.

We went into his bathroom (not before he grabbed his extender), and he fucked me on the bathroom counter.

As I began to cum from his "dick," he got down on his knees and lapped up all the wetness I had produced—building the waves higher and higher to crash over me again.

After a fight with my lover's wife, a full day and night of work, and three orgasms later, I was exhausted. I almost fell asleep in the bathroom.

"You must be tired. Come on, let's go lay down." Thierry scooped me up like a child and placed me in his bed, but I was asleep before he could get around to the other side.

The last thing I remembered thinking was, *This man is gonna fuck me in as many corners of the globe as physically possible...and I'm up for the challenge!*

Sixteen

Waking up the following day to an empty bed and a mostly quiet house was a bit unnerving for me. Trying to make myself look and feel like a human again, I went to the adjoining restroom to wash my face and brush my teeth. I saw a toothbrush on top of a post-it with my name on it and a smiley face. Thierry had thought of everything, and that level of detailed attention made me smile from the inside. This trip was going to be the time of my life.

I heard humming, so I went into the kitchen to say good morning. Brandon was there in a tank top and jeans. He was facing the sink, and I could finally see all the muscles his suits barely covered. He felt me behind him and looked over his shoulder, smiling.

"Good morning, miss."

I wonder if he saw the lust in my eyes.

"Good morning, Brandon. It's so weird to see you in regular clothes. To what do we owe this occasion?"

"Mr. Jorrington caught his flight soon after you fell asleep last night, so I can dress however I like until I am at his service again."

It felt like I was wearing nothing the way he was looking at me. I swore he could see through my clothes.

"So," he started as he drank his freshly squeezed juice, "have you decided whether or not you will accompany Mr. Jorrington?" He passed me a glass of my own and a croissant for which I was grateful. My stomach was growling like crazy.

"I've decided to go. Assuming my job will let me off for that long. I mean, what do I have to lose?"

"What indeed? It is the opportunity of a lifetime, and I, of course, plan to join you both once I get a week or so off to visit family."

My phone started pinging, so I ran back to my purse to retrieve it, interrupting our conversation.

"It's Thierry!" I squealed, ignoring all the other messages from Darrell.

Today 9:16 AM

Thierry: You looked so peaceful sleeping, I couldn't bear to wake you. By the time you read this, I'll be in the air somewhere headed home to London. Once you decide what day you'd like to come see me, please, message Brandon, and he will make the accommodations for you. You were the best thing about this trip to New York, and I hope to see you soon...xo, Thierry.

"Well, apparently, I'm supposed to get in touch with you when I decide on the day I can leave," I said to Brandon, looking up from my phone.

"Yes, ma'am. You have my contact information, right?"

"I do. Thank you for everything you've done for me so far; I will definitely be in touch."

I started gathering my things to get ready to go, and I felt his eyes on my body. Why was it turning me on so much, and why would Thierry leave me alone with his *fine*-ass butler?

"Brandon?" I heard a woman's voice call out, drowsily. "Brandon, where is my juice…come back to bed. I need you."

"…coming, love."

I looked away, embarrassed. I was having such lustful thoughts about Brandon when he clearly already had someone in his bed waiting for him.

"You and I will be spending quite a bit of time together while we're overseas. If there's anything I can do to make you more comfortable, promise me that you'll let me know."

"I will, Brandon. Thank you." I grabbed my coat and walked out into the night air, grateful I stayed in my lane. He was clearly just an employee of Thierry's and wanted to make sure that I was okay—nothing more; nothing less.

Although it was early, I thought about calling Darrell. Instead of calling him back, I just read his texts over and over, trying to decipher what was true and what continued to be deception.

Today 9:34 AM

Darrell: Nik, I'm sorry. I didn't mean for any of this to happen.

Darrell: You are something truly special to me, and I fucked up...on more than one occasion. But you know as well as I do that we have something between us. It's not regular. It's not common—it's extraordinary, and that doesn't come around every day...at least, not for me. Please, give me a chance to explain.

I deleted the message, deciding to take the long way home to think.

Seventeen

On Monday around mid-morning, Emily invited me into her office and offered me a full-time position with full benefits. I nearly cried, as I would be making $2k more than I had initially budgeted for.

"Emily, this offer is almost too good to be true—of course, I accept! I-I just have one thing I'd like to negotiate with you."

"I'm so proud of you for negotiating," she whispered. Then, it was back to her regular voice. "What you got?" she smiled.

I took a deep breath, and before I could lose my courage, I said, "I'd like to delay my start date for at least six-weeks while I take care of a few personal things…would that be possible?"

Emily sat back in her chair.

"Six-weeks is a long time, *[redacted]*." She thought silently, tapping her pen on the desk. "You know what…? I'm about to take a two-week vacation during our slow season…how about if you're gone during those two-weeks and the two-weeks following for a total of four-weeks? That way, you can train the interns on what to do in your absence, and I can have two-weeks without you here to form a plan-of-action for you when you return. So, four-weeks?" She stood to her feet and offered me her hand with a warm smile.

"It's a deal!" I said, shaking her hand probably too vigorously.

"Well, I leave next Monday. So as your last act as an intern, take the week to train the others, and…well, I don't have to tell you how to do that. You're a *natural* manager. I trust that it will get done." She put on her glasses and swiveled back around to her computer. "Welcome aboard! HR has your paperwork ready to sign. I'll adjust your start date to four-weeks from next Monday."

I couldn't tell if my heart was beating fast from the job offer, the rush of negotiations, or the excitement for how spot-on Thierry was about requesting time off. Either way, I raced to a restroom to call him. I didn't care what time it was in London.

He answered on the second ring.

"Sexy, how are you? I can't talk long. I'm getting on the tube."

"I just wanted you to hear my voice when I told you I took the job—with a month off! I'll text Brandon to set up a flight."

"That is fabulous news—I cannot wait to see you. There's so much fun to be had. Talk to you soon, love."

After texting Brandon, I started to formulate a plan for the other interns to take my place. I honestly didn't know if they were aware of all I did around the office, but they were about to find out. If they missed a step in my absence, it wouldn't be my problem after Friday.

Brandon texted me right back, asking for my passport information and told me to be packed Saturday night for a red-eye out of JFK.

I screamed into my hands.

Life was good, and I was going to milk *every* minute of it.

Eighteen

I barely remembered coming home from work. It was like I floated home on a cloud of excitement of what was to come.

When I arrived home, parked outside my building was a white-on-white 745 BMW. I instantly could feel my high coming down as I dealt with the reality of Darrell's fine-ass getting out of the car to greet me.

"Can I come up…?" He was dressed in gray joggers and sneakers. I wasn't sure how he managed to make that shit look classy, but he did. And he always smelled clean, yet sexy—like he wore a scent with the same base, but the notes changed every time I saw him.

"Do you have someone who makes a mix of essential oils for your specific pheromones or something?" I asked, completely ignoring his question.

He smiled.

"Yes, I do. He's on 125th Street I can take you there right now…I think he's still open. Hold on." Darrell quickly pulled out his phone. "Abdul, are you at the spot? For how long…? Okay, I'm leaving 145th now. Can you make something special when I get there, or are you on your way out? Okay, I'm on my way—for a woman. No, not her…just wait; I'll be there soon."

I didn't say a word. I just hopped in the passenger seat, and he sped off driving South toward 125th Street, arguably Harlem's busiest street.

Darrell had what sounded like a playlist of Drake's saddest songs pumping through the speakers as we drove in silence. 125th Street was packed for a Monday, but he double-parked right between 7th and Lenox, across from the State Building. I had walked past this place a million-times and never noticed it before. There was a narrow door leading to an even narrower staircase, going up what felt like two-flights. The scents coming from this mystery place were heavenly. My nose knew we had arrived before my eyes because the scents were only getting stronger.

At the top of the stairs was a wooden door and a peephole. Darrell knocked on the door, and whoever was on the other side quickly opened up.

"My guy!"

"The Mad Scientist! What's good, baby?!" They slapped hands and greeted each other with a hug. "Abdul, this is [*redacted*]. This woman is very special to me," he said, as his eyes locked with mine, "and I need her to trust me, so I'm opening up my world to her…in *any* way she requests—and even the ways she hasn't yet."

Abdul was a tall Middle Eastern man dressed in what appeared to be traditional garb. He had spiky hair and a nicely groomed 5 o'clock shadow. His hands were soft, and he had rings on nearly every finger. I could tell English was not his first language, but I had no problem understanding him.

The inside of this place was dimly lit with a really sexy vibe—and it smelled *amazing,* but not like your regular mall fragrance shop or even an incense store. If *exclusivity* had a smell, it would be this.

The wood panel floor shined like it was taken care of daily, and there were glass beakers with different color liquids inside each one lining the walls.

"Abdul provides the oils for most of the guys you see outside peddling the usual scents—*Black Love, Sex on the Beach,* and the ones that imitate actual perfumes—his nose is highly sought after. He doesn't typically take walk-ins, but…"

"But," Abdul interrupted, "when you have a friend-turned-client who has supported you over ten-years through good and bad, you do not say, 'no.'" They smiled as though they were true friends who had known one another for years.

Abdul turned to me.

"So, what kind of fragrance are you looking for?"

"Honestly, I didn't know I was shopping for a fragrance today. I just love how Darrell always smells, I don't know…like himself—like the *best* version of himself. Maybe, it has his pheromones in it or something?"

He smiled.

"It does actually. And the process may seem *odd* to you at first, but the results speak for themselves."

Abdul went into a drawer and got out a long Q-tip and a pair of latex gloves. It looked like the kind doctors use during a pap smear. I'm sure my face reflected my confusion because they both started laughing.

"Yes, it's exactly what you think it is. Well, perhaps, not *exactly* what you think…anyway, we have to find a scent you actually like first, so let's focus on that," Abdul said matter-of-factly, asking me what basic scents I already liked in order to get a scent profile on me.

After fooling around with sandalwood, vanilla, and ylang ylang, I settled on a scent that made a pretty color and smelled amazing. I asked Darrell if he liked how it smelled, and he looked intoxicated. I couldn't tell if he was putting on or not, but I was pleased with my choice.

"Now, go into the restroom, wash your hands, put on these gloves, retrieve some of the secretions from your flower bomb and drop it into the machine there. You'll know it when you see it."

"My-My 'flower bomb'?" I stuttered, making sure we were using the same euphemism.

Darrell held me close and whispered in my ear, "Do you want me to help you get your juices flowing?" while Abdul looked away, chuckling.

Standing that close to him already activated my body even though he had lied to me over and over again.

"No, no, I got it," I said, pulling away. I was ashamed because I knew my body was going to betray me. I could feel it.

Looking doubtful, I took the swab and walked into the bright, clinical-looking restroom, and did as I was told. The machine Abdul was talking about looked like a *smell-o-meter* or something. It sucked the Q-tip into itself and started swirling around and making a loud humming noise.

"Hurry and come out so you can see what you created!" I heard Darrell say excitedly. I pulled my panties up and hurried out.

The machine was connected on the outside by tubing, and the perfume I had created was sitting underneath. As soon as I exited the restroom, Darrell was behind me.

"I wish I could fill a bottle with the scent of your pussy," he said, and I felt my knees weaken along with my resolve to hate his lying-ass.

Three little drops of pussy juice came from the tube-like condensation and dropped right into the vial the perfume was in. Abdul had on gloves and goggles by this point. He mixed the mixture together, and the color changed. He topped it, labeled it *Control,* and handed it to me.

"Use with caution. You'll be pretty much irresistible smelling like this," he said with a twinkle in his eye.

Once we were finished, I saw Darrell peel off three $100 bills before we said our goodbyes.

"This oil cost $300?! Get the fuck outta here," I whispered on the stairs, as we headed down to his car.

"Actually, it costs more than that, but I get a discount," he laughed. "It's worth it though, right? I mean, for that eccentric experience?"

"I guess."

"I remember meeting Abdul in undergrad. He was a chemistry major there on full-scholarship. He was essentially a genius. But during junior year, he dropped out of college. Everyone thought he was crazy, but not me. I started calling him, 'The Mad Scientist,' would check-up on him, and fed him every now and then...even helped him get the capital for his business. You see, Abdul is the truth!"

I dabbed some of the scent behind my ear before hopping back into his car, heading straight to my house. Darrell parked on a side street, and it was pretty dark, so I decided to satiate the desire I had to swallow his big-ass dick. Maybe, the smell of my own pheromones was turning me on, but I knew I had to get some more of him before I left for London.

Before he parked, I started rubbing his knee and thigh, hoping to run into his dick with my hand, but he had it on his left-side, so I couldn't get to it. It was like he had read my mind because as soon as he parked, he pulled my face close to his and kissed me hard and deep while he pulled his dick out with his other hand. I grabbed it and moaned. The weight of it alone turned me on even more, causing me to salivate.

Darrell pulled away breathlessly.

"Nik, why you want me so bad? Why? I can't get enough of you, and it seems like it's the same for you. What could it possibly be about the two of us…?"

Before he could say another word, I gobbled his dick up, damn-near saturating the top of his sweats with my spit. While his dick was in my mouth, I reached into my pants and sure enough, I was slimy wet. I started playing with my clit while he was down my throat, which was not an easy task in the front seat of a luxury vehicle, but I couldn't help myself.

"It's…oh, baby, baby. Keep doing that shit with your tongue." I felt him stiffen.

"Your mouth feels too good, I-I-I can't hold back," and just like that, he came in my mouth—much faster than I had anticipated. I almost forgot how good my head game was.

Darrell's climax initiated my own. I was right behind him, clenching around my own fingers moments later, thankful I didn't squirt all over his leather seats.

I rolled down the window and spit his spunk out.

He had his tongue back down my throat before I could get the window all the way up.

"Let's go upstairs," he said, between kisses.

We were giggling walking into the building arm-in-arm when I saw G. Money posted up at the entrance to the building.

"Wassup, young blood?" Darrell said to him as he walked by with a smirk. He could probably tell that G. Money had tried to get with me by how he was scowling at him. But who knows…maybe he could tell that G. Money and I had done all kinds of nasty things together.

"Wassup, G., you good?" I asked. He looked *big* mad. Honestly, I had been dodging him and his texts for the past few weeks now. I mean, juggling two dicks was enough.

"Wassup, O.G.?" G. Money ice grilled us as we walked by, and I swore I could feel his eyes in the back of my head.

That little interaction didn't matter though. Darrell and I both stripped and were all over each other before the front door even closed. I loved his body—how it wasn't super muscular like Thierry's. He clearly worked out, but his idea of healthy wasn't about protein shakes and reps. He was a little soft in the middle and strong up top.

"Please, tell me I didn't use the last condom the other day," Darrell said, checking his pockets.

"*Fuck!* I think we did."

"Okay. I'll be right back…are you allergic to anything? I mean, is latex okay? Should I be looking for…like sheepskin or some shit?" he asked, throwing his clothes on quickly.

I just laughed.

"Darrell, get some regular-ass latex condoms, please. And hurry," I said, smacking his ass. "I need you inside me *noooowwww.*"

After he left for the store, I decided to put on my Chillhop playlist and light a few candles…might as well make our last time a good one since I would be leaving the country soon and quitting Dream.

I walked slowly to the restroom to make sure I looked okay and tucked away my new body oil for safekeeping. My heart was racing with anticipation, and I felt myself smiling from ear-to-ear, despite the fact that Darrell was a huge liar. There was just *something* so sexy about him that I couldn't really pinpoint.

I looked at myself in the mirror and remembered that my underwear didn't match, and there was even a chance my panties had a hole in them. I began to panic, hoping I had enough time to change clothes before Darrell returned. I frantically went through my wardrobe mentally—both the things I had worn to work (where Darrell had seen me most frequently) and what I had that matched in my tiny closet. The issue was that most of my clothing budget was spent either on new clothes for the club or vintage items for Bel—I had rarely tried to impress anyone with my underwear, so I usually didn't spend a lot of money on them. Typically, just getting naked did the trick when I was with a suitor I wanted to bed.

I stripped naked and started trying on things that looked like I either was *really* trying or not trying at all.

Ugh, being a woman is such hard work!

I didn't realize how much pussy residue I was leaving behind on everything until I went to try something back on, and it was already wet, thanks to Darrell's kisses from earlier.

Thinking about his dick in my mouth was making me even more wet, and I had to pull myself from the reverie when I heard my buzzer, indicating he was downstairs.

"Fuck!" I said loudly, after buzzing him in. Then, I remembered my Halloween costume from last year and hurried to squeeze myself into a bright yellow body con dress. I went to a party with four friends as the Fanta girls, and I was Pineapple Fanta. The yellow was so bright I could never wear it again alone, but with it hiked up enough for my ass cheeks to show and no panties on, it would do the trick.

"What took you so long…? I missed you," I said, unbuckling his belt and nibbling on his ear as soon as Darrell walked through the door.

"People are crazy out there, Nik. There was a fight in front of the spot, so I waited until it cleared out. I'm just tryna stay outta trouble, you know? You really need to think about getting out of this area…"

I just nodded, licking his neck as he moaned. He pulled me off him and looked me in the eyes.

"Make sure you stay inside unless you're coming or going. We have to take care of this body, okay? Your block can be dangerous…wait, what do you have on?" His eyes got big, and I knew I had chosen well. He was parched, looking at me like a real bottle of soda.

"I'll be right back," he gasped, kissing me fully and running to the bathroom. "Don't move. I just need to wash my hands before I touch you." Within moments, he came back and growled in my ear. "You look good enough to eat," he said while grabbing my left ass cheek.

Using his longest finger to do the things his dick could not, he pleasured my pussy as he leaned over to kiss my neck and ear, feeling me throb. Pulling my breasts out of my dress, he gave each one the attention it needed before he grabbed them both and put my nipples in his mouth at the same time. I couldn't tell which moans were mine and which were his, as I felt the pressure inside me rise.

He grabbed my face and licked my lips.

"Do you want to cum on my dick…or my face?" he whispered.

He spun me around to face my front door and dropped to his knees, licking, and sucking on every inch of my body, taking his time savoring the flavor that was me.

By the time he entered me, I was already gushing—accepting his dick with just a bit of hesitation into every corner of my love box. His manhood tested my boundary of pain and pleasure; he was so big I wasn't sure if I could accommodate every position he wanted to try.

When he flipped me over to bite my ass and tossed a pillow underneath my pelvis, I felt myself getting dick-matized by this man. He crossed my feet at the ankles and made sure that the pillow was positioned under my groin. Entering me from behind like that made me even tighter for his fully grown dick and gave him full access to my g-spot. I came twice from that position alone. During my second orgasm, he pulled out quickly, lifted my ass to his mouth, and began licking me from front to back—giving me tingles I had never ever felt before.

When he sat cross-legged and pulled me on top of him, I felt him getting closer to the finish line, so I started riding him like a bull, forcing him to cum for me.

"…I'm cumming, for you," he yelled before he pulled me close, breathing heavily.

He grabbed my face immediately and began kissing me deeply, telling me he loved me.

Pulling away, I tried not to act any differently and just chalked it up to the rantings of a man high on orgasmic oxytocin.

Nineteen

"So, you own Dream, you're married…I just fucked a *liar* like he was my man. What the fuck is wrong with me?"

"Yes, I own Dream. I'm not a manager there. Yes, I'm *un*happily married. And yes, I know we have something special…what else do you want to know?"

We talked for hours, going down a list of trivial and thought-provoking questions we somehow never got around to in our many talks at the club. We had discussed so many things about what made us who we are without even talking about who we *actually* were. I couldn't blame him completely for the deception, but I knew trusting him again wouldn't be easy.

Could I even seriously date a married man? Was I really considering it? What is so special about him that would make me deny the sanctity of marriage?

These were too many questions for a Monday, seriously.

"Hey, I'm starving. Are you hungry?" Darrell asked. "How about Chinese? I know a cool spot nearby. I can bring us some back."

"That sounds perfect," I agreed, and he called in the order while getting dressed.

A knock on my door ten-minutes after he left surprised me.

"How'd you get the food that fast?" I laughed, as I opened the door without looking.

G. Money was standing there.

"I don't have no food, but you definitely got something I could eat."

He was rubbing his hands together, licking his lips.

"Boy, if you don't..." I tried to close the door in his face, but he put his arm up to stop me.

"[*Redacted*], Darrell ain't who you think he is. You probably got with him because you think he got money, and he does—*long* money—but he's a dirtbag. That's why we call him 'D. Bag'."

Now, it was my turn to scowl at him.

"Nigga, get the fuck outta here! And who is 'we'...?" My curiosity had always been stronger than my anger.

G. Money laughed, but there was no humor in his eyes.

"He's hella connected in Harlem. Everybody knows him for a reason. He was probably my supplier's supplier. Hell, he probably still is. He is a stone-cold killer and a dirtbag who will do anything for a dime...or if he thinks you've done him wrong. Rumor is, he sent his own wife to the track when he was low on funds once. I'm sure you've caught him in a lie or two by now, and you're a dumb bitch if you believe anything he says."

"Ya' mama's a dumb bitch!" I screamed.

I hadn't seen or heard Darrell come down the hallway, and apparently G. Money didn't either, because Darrell walked up behind him, startling us both.

"Hey, young blood. It looks like the lady doesn't wanna speak to you. Would you kindly return to your own place?"

G. Money immediately tried to go, but Darrell put him in some kind of police hold without dropping our food.

"Whatever you said to her made her upset, so on second thought, just don't talk to her anymore…aye, *aye,* stop struggling. I'ma let you go…" Darrel was speaking so calmly it was eerie.

"It's cool, O.G. It's cool. You right. I'ma go. Y'all be cool."

Darrell closed the door, still holding the food.

"Are you okay?" he asked.

I wasn't sure if I wanted to disclose all that G. Money had said to me—nor was I sure how much he had heard, so I said, "Yeah, I'm okay. He's a dope boy I used to fuck wit', acting kinda crazy now."

Despite my response, my mind was racing.

I had no idea what was real and what was fabricated by G. Money.

How does he know Darrell's name if they aren't involved somehow? How does he know Darrell's a liar? Is he really a drug dealer…?

Darrell never discussed how he made his money…was it through the drug game? The most disconcerting part was when G. Money said, *"he is a stone-cold killer."* I had joked with myself that Thierry was "The Killer," but did I have my antennae up on the wrong person?

I quickly banished those thoughts because I knew I was a good judge of character. Surely, all this time in strip clubs had given me some sort of discernment.

Darrell didn't seem too concerned.

"I figured he'd tasted some of that good pussy at some point. He'd be a fool not to *try,* at least. Honestly, Nik, you got a lot to go crazy over, and that's keeping it a buck. If you did even *half* the shit with him that you do with me, I would be knocking down your door too." He sat down, opening the food and serving us both. "It's probably about time I help you get out of this building anyway. What you think?"

"*Welllllll,*" I said, "funny you should say that because I got a job offer today at my internship, so, maybe, I'll actually be able to afford a building with a doorman…or at least, a lobby that doesn't reek of urine."

"Why didn't you tell me?! Congratulations!" He twirled me around. "See, I knew there was a reason I stopped to get this bubbly." He reached in his bag and pulled out a bottle of Veuve Clicquot Rosé.

I quickly hugged him.

"You got this just *because*?"

"I wanted to toast to the start of a new beginning with you and me—but now, we have two things to toast to!"

By this time, my conversation with G. Money was completely forgotten.

I had a lot on my mind, but the bubbles from the champagne mixed with the good company and supreme pussy licking compartmentalized those things, and put them away on a shelf, not to be thought of again until the following day.

Twenty

Darrell left a little before midnight, being transparent about going home to his family, and I was grateful for the time alone. I twisted the cap on my new body oil, inhaling deeply, and started trying to figure out what the hell I was doing with my love life. Sleeping with and possibly falling for a married man had never been on my bucket list, but here we were—and honestly…I felt no guilt about it.

I wasn't sure if I was willing to overlook his marriage because of Danielle's mental health issues or just because our connection was so incredibly strong.

This was the *most* selfish thing I had ever done—not caring at all about the feelings of another woman. Either I was sacrificing my moral compass, or my heart had grown cold. It felt like Darrell and me had been through so much together in such a small amount of time. So, watching him open up to me was like a true metamorphosis. It was rare to find someone with as much to offer as Darrell did—I mean, who would accept me for being a sex worker, gyrating on men all night long? But on the other hand, Thierry had accepted it without a second thought…maybe, it was my own midwestern, puritanical hang-ups about sex that led me to believe more men would discount my "value" based on my career choice.

Either way it went, Darrell knew the ins-and-outs of what I did and had accepted it seemingly with no judgement. Not to mention how much of a gentleman he was and how he always went out of his way to make me feel special.

Drinking the last of the champagne, my mind then wandered to the conversation I'd had with G. Money. What did he mean by the term, "D-bag"? And was that stuff true that Darrell had set his own wife out for money?

I wanted to text G. Money, but I was sure that he was probably embarrassed after getting hemmed up like that.

Today 12:14 AM

Me: Hey, G, sorry about tonight. Um, can we talk more about what you were saying about Darrell sometime this week?

G. Money: I don't think that's a good idea.

Me: I just want to hear more about what you were saying. I don't appreciate you calling me a "dumb bitch," and I know Darrell had no right to put his hands on you, but you were being a complete asshole. I'll give you a call tomorrow sometime.

G. Money: ...

I saw that he was replying, so I went to wash my face and brush my teeth, anticipating a response from him when I got back to my bedroom.

As I finished up in the bathroom, suddenly, I heard a gunshot go off—but I didn't pay it any mind. Maybe, it *was* time to move into a building with more safety. I had a lot to think about, and I was grateful that I had less than a week before I would be boarding my flight to London.

Checking my phone, it looked like G. Money was still replying—I fell asleep with the phone in my hand waiting for his response.

When I woke up, I saw no text from G. Money, but I figured I would just give him a call later, regardless of what he said.

The rest of the week passed with a blur and the news of my promotion traveled fast.

I received congratulatory flowers and candy from my family back home, Darrell, *and* Thierry. Thierry's was just signed: *We'll celebrate properly when I see you in a few days...xo,* so I knew it was from him—and his thoughtfulness made me smile.

As far as Darrell went, he was busy most nights being a dad and all, which was fine with me. He texted me all-day to check on me and gave me the attention I needed even if I was unable to see him in-person. He didn't know I was leaving, and I didn't plan to tell him until I was checking-in at JFK.

I was too busy trying to figure out what to do with my life and make sure my plants wouldn't die while I was gone to stress about the attention of a man with an *entire* family.

I took some time from being boy-crazy to just walk around New York, specifically, Harlem, enjoying the beautiful chaos, the brown faces, the history, the vibrations. Despite being from Kansas City, Missouri, there was no place I wanted to call home more than Harlem.

Brandon sent me all the information I would need for my flight—and his, since we were on the same flight to Heathrow. He was very helpful in choosing what to bring.

"Pack comfortable clothes, underwear, and workout gear. I'm sure Mr. Jorrington already has a full wardrobe for you. And if he doesn't, I'm sure he's already set you up with a personal shopper. So, I wouldn't worry about bringing too much, miss! Let's not forget what industry you're both in…"

"FASHION!" we said, at the same time, laughing.

A shopping spree upon arrival definitely sounded *heavenly.*

I worked at the club on Thursday and Friday, unsure *if* or *when* I would be working there again. Those were the best nights, partially because the pressure to make money wasn't really there. I just danced and had a good time…I even had a drink.

I didn't tell anyone I was leaving, but they may have guessed something was shifting in my life by my actions. I just quietly cleaned out my locker and took my things home after my shift Friday night.

Saturday, Darrell texted me to ask if I wanted to go to brunch, but I told him that I already had plans—and I did! I took myself out to brunch, and I people-watched, still soaking up the energy of the city.

I couldn't believe my good fortune—I was healthy, *mostly* happy, a recipient of regular great sex, about to travel and see the world, returning to a great job in an industry I had loved ever since I was a girl. I tried not waiting for the other shoe to drop, but I couldn't help thinking that it would…eventually.

After I got home, I took a nap and got my things together for the airport. Then, I finally texted Darrell.

Today 11:37 PM

Me: Hey, sorry I was unable to meet today. I'm leaving the country for a few weeks and may be unreachable. Be well...and maybe, I'll see you when I return? Xo

I immediately saw that he was typing a response.

Darrell: Wait. What? You're leaving? Damn, now I regret not seeing you this week. When I saw you Monday, you knew you were going and didn't say anything? I guess I deserve that. I likely deserve more than that to be honest. Have fun and, please, let me know that you've arrived safely; you are precious cargo, my dear.

That made me smile.

My stomach began to flutter as we pulled into my gate at JFK. I got my bag out of the trunk, checked into my flight, and saw Brandon in the TSA pre-check line *way* ahead of me. He must've felt me looking at the back of his head because he turned around and waved, mouthing, *"See you at the gate."*

I was nervous to be on such a long flight at first, meeting a man I had only really known for a week, but seeing Brandon made me feel at ease.

After buying a bottle of water and making my way to the gate, I spotted an empty seat and grabbed it—then stood up to look for Brandon. He was across the way with his headphones on and his eyes closed.

I opened my book and settled in, waiting for our gate to open, glancing up every now and then at the TV above me.

For some reason, I looked up at the local news and saw a face I recognized—Darrell's!

"Local man, Darrell 'D. Bag' Hutchins, accused of attempted murder in the first degree. This video shows him allegedly shooting a tenant at this apartment complex, a low-level drug dealer by the name of Gerald 'G. Money' Mooney. Hutchins has been arrested many times, but never charged. He has been taken into custody while Gerald remains in critical condition at Harlem Hospital."

I sat, staring at the television screen, not realizing that I wasn't breathing. My mind kept replaying the grainy video that looked exactly like Darrell…shooting G. Money.

"*Now boarding Gate B17 to Heathrow—our first-class passengers are welcome to board.*" The announcement shook me back to reality. I hadn't looked at my boarding pass, so I didn't realize that I was first-class until I saw Brandon motioning for me to join him in line.

I must've looked like a zombie, as he looked truly concerned.

"Are you okay?"

"Yes, of course. Why do you ask?" I responded, taking a sip of water, trying to bring the color back to my face.

"You look like you just saw a ghost," he said as we scanned our boarding passes and walked onto the jetway.

"Yes, I…the book I'm reading just got *real* is all."

"Okay, well, as long as you're okay." He didn't sound too convinced. "Do you want the window or the aisle?"

"Whichever is fine, honestly. I didn't even realize that I was in first-class. This is my first time."

Placing my carry-on in the bin above me, my mind was still in a bit of a fog. *Was it true? Did Darrell really try to kill G. Money?* I guess, I really was a "dumb bitch" after all. *Should I be talking to the police?* I was getting on an international flight just five-days after an attempted murder took place and I knew both parties…*does this look like something a guilty person would do*? I started breathing hard. Brandon must've thought I was having a panic attack or something.

"It's okay, just breathe. We'll be there before you know it." He was being so kind.

"Thank you. I'm-I'm okay—I love flying. I just…I need to visit the restroom."

Before I could get up, my phone started buzzing in my hand.

The caller ID said, "Private," so I let it go to voicemail.

By the time I got to the restroom, I saw that I had a message.

Sitting down to compose myself, I read the transcript.

Missed Call /Visual Voicemail

Today 7:39 PM

Private: "[Redacted], this is Detective Blancocci."

Private: "We need to speak with you about your text messages to Gerald Mooney in regard to Darrell Hutchinson—they were the last ones he received. Please, give us a call back at (212) 690-6311. Thank you."

I splashed my face with some cool water, took three deep breaths, and then returned to my seat. After putting my phone to *airplane mode,* I decided to just go to sleep—maybe, this would all go away by the time I woke up in London…

Stay Tuned for *Nikki Chronicles II*…

About the Author

Meet Cherayla…a self-described "fake-foodie" who knows good music when she hears it.

Cherayla's characters can be found acting out scenes in her mind at any given time since they have been living full lives in her head for over a decade waiting for her to give them life.

While Nikki Chronicles is Cherayla's debut novel, it will be released as a trilogy and there are many other projects on the horizon, so stay tuned!

Stay Connected with Cherayla!

Link: www.linktr.ee/cherayla

Made in the USA
Monee, IL
03 August 2023

40425931R10105